WHEN A LIGER MATES

A LION'S PRIDE #10

EVE LANGLAIS

A
LION'S
PRIDE
THE SERIES

CHAPTER ONE

Thick fingers adorned in chunky rings stroked the fur of the giant feline leashed by his side. Guillaume Champignon had certain hobbies. Collecting large and rare wild animals—and training them to obey him—was one of them.

"Are we on track for the hunt?" Guillaume asked of the woman standing in front of his desk, her hair cut blunt and streaked with gray.

Tracey held up a tablet and slid her finger across it, the light from the screen illuminating her face. "Everything is a go for tonight's entertainment."

"We have enough prey?" His fingers stilled on the large cat's head. It had gone stiff. It made no sound, and yet he could have sworn the liger vibrated. It had better not be growling without permission. His kennel master had assured him the beast was quite tame.

"We have more than plenty, with two to spare."

"Good." Nothing worse than when a client finished the hunt unsatisfied because they didn't bag anything.

"I don't pay to leave empty handed," one of Guillaume's most generous guests had once exclaimed. Those paying for the privilege expected a trophy.

They also weren't picky about what they shot. The accident on the last hunt had cost him a chunk of his profits to cover it up.

Somehow, a woman had wandered onto the secured property. Went gallivanting through the woods on a night the hunters were set loose. It was an easy mistake to make. The hunters all wore bright fluorescents, whereas the intruder appeared to be trespassing naked as the day she was born.

The bullet went through her stomach, and while she was alive when his wardens got to her, it was a deadly wound. A nearby river took care of the remains.

Which left only the client who shot her. Rewinding through the footage that tracked the hunter and prey, they could see who'd been in that sector just before the kill.

Bernard, a low-end client, claimed innocence. He tried to convince them he'd shot a lioness, except their tracking data showed no one near him. It cost Bernard a large sum to keep his mistake secret. And even after he paid, Guillaume had him taken out as an example to anyone else that thought to jeopardize his operation.

An oddity about the whole mess was they did come across a discarded tracking bracelet in the woods—for a lioness as a matter of fact, a feline who'd disappeared without a trace.

"I hear we have a few lionesses this time," Guillaume

mused aloud. Quite a few, considering they mostly managed to capture bears and wolves.

"Three, all brought in last night."

"Did another illegal zoo get raided?" Animals for the hunt weren't easy to come by. Either they poached them illegally or purchased them from a collector thinning their herd.

"Private owner. Claimed he was remodeling and needed to get rid of them." Tracey dropped her arm with the tablet practically attached at the end down to her side.

"His loss, our gain." A distant sound caught his attention. Guillaume strained to listen. "Did you hear something?"

Tracey turned to look over her shoulder. "Is that gunfire?"

Removing his fingers from the tense hairs on his cat, Guillaume stood. He braced his hands on his desk, opening the line to his secretary. "Cirine, what's going on?"

Usually the height of efficiency, his secretary didn't reply.

The popping sounds stopped abruptly, only to be replaced with a roar.

A second blood-chilling snarl followed.

Then a third.

What the ever-loving fuck was going on?

Grawr.

Was that a freaking wolf? In his lodge?

It sounded as if his menagerie had gotten loose.

Unlikely, and yet he leaned over to open the drawer of his desk. Reached for—

Nothing. He gaped at the empty space. No gun.

There was a sudden staccato of gunfire, then a muffled yell, followed by a roar, then nothing.

Eyes wide enough to pop, Tracey hugged her tablet and backed toward the wall farthest from the door. She appeared fixated by it.

The urge was understandable. Guillaume stared, too. Held his breath at the silence beyond it.

What was going on?

A shift of fur and muscle drew his attention to the forgotten feline by his side. A massive beast. Part lion, part tiger. A liger as they called these kinds of hybrids. And already so tame.

It was sent to him as a gift only a day ago. He'd been amazed at how well it obeyed commands, even as he scorned how meek the creature was.

It didn't appear subservient at the moment. It sat on its haunches, and Guillaume would have sworn it smiled.

It definitely winked.

Guillaume found it hard to control the tremble in his muscles as it stood, stretched. Then suddenly it wasn't a liger anymore but a big man with a shaggy head of hair. A naked man.

"Who are you?" Guillaume managed to exclaim.

"You may call me Law. Cousin to the young woman you tried to murder last month."

"I don't know what you're talking about," Guillaume blubbered. What was happening? How could this man be the liger he'd been petting only minutes ago? Sweat rolled down his temple and dripped off his cheek.

"I know what you're doing here." The man who called himself Law stepped forward.

"I don't care what you think you know. You're trespassing. My guards will shoot you if I ask."

"What guards?" Law took a step forward, his eyes intent and deadly. "Let's play a game, Guillaume. A game of the hunter and the hunted. Guess which one you're going to be."

"But you're not human. That's not fair," Guillaume sputtered.

"And you're going to tell me that the slaughter you've arranged here is fair?" Law smiled. Guillaume's bladder constricted. "Payback's a bitch. Are you ready to run for your life?" The blond goliath rolled his head, cracking his spine. Shrugged his shoulders.

"You can't do this." Guillaume had begun to hyperventilate.

Law stood still. "Five, four, three—"

The countdown spurred Guillaume into action. He ran for the patio doors leading onto the balcony. Surely there was someone on duty who could shoot the intruder.

As he emerged onto the terrace, three lions swaggered into view. Big. Tawny. And staring at his juicy ass.

"Fuck me!" he wheezed.

But it was only when they shifted in a way his mind refused to grasp, and stood as naked women, that he pissed himself.

·   ·   ·

AN HOUR LATER, basking in the heat of the flames crackling from the lodge...

"I hate it when they pee themselves." His aunt Lenore was the one to start the lament. "Way too easy to track. Takes all the fun out of it."

"Not to mention who wants to touch them once they're marinating in it," Aunt Lacey declared, having already donned her one-piece pantsuit.

Lawrence wore a pair of pants and not much else as he watched the lodge burn. There would be no more hunts, not here at any rate, but fighting poachers remained a full-time job.

Aunt Lena, who was quite fond of cousin Miriam—the one shot and dumped in a river—stood by his side. "Miri is going to be pissed we took care of this without her."

"We couldn't wait, and she needed more time to recover." Because his cousin had almost died. Being a lion shifter made her strong, but even they had to give themselves time to heal.

"I am hungry," Lenore announced. "Bring on the meat."

"I know a place," Lacey declared.

"Does it offer only fake meat?" Lena asked with a scowl. "I don't want any of that weird vegan stuff."

"It's not weird. It's choosing to not eat possible distant family members."

"I am not related to cows. And even if I were, I'd still eat them because they're delicious." A deliberate jibe.

"Savage." Lacey's lips pursed, and Lena flexed for battle.

It happened all too often. He stepped between his aunts.

"Now, ladies," he chastised.

Aunt Lena shoved him out of the way. "We don't need you getting involved, squirt."

Squirt.

They still treated him like a child. "I'm a grown man," he declared.

"Really? I couldn't tell on account you're still getting into trouble." That was a matter-of-fact statement from Lenore.

"I don't know what you mean," he blustered.

"Ahem." Aunt Lacey cleared her throat. "The incident with the Russians."

"Was fixed without incident."

"Only by accident. What about the Canadian-border thing a few months ago?" Aunt Lenore had one of those memories that could bring up every wrong thing he'd ever done.

"A misunderstanding." Apparently having sex in the interview rooms was a no-no.

"You need a keeper," Aunt Lacey stated.

"Not us," piped in Aunt Lenore. "No offense, you're like a son to me, but it's time someone else took on the task."

"I don't need a keeper. I'm thirty-five years old. I am a well-regarded member of the Pride."

"And it's past time you settled down and got domestic," Lacey replied pertly.

"None of you ever did," he pointed out.

"Because I didn't need a keeper," Lena pointed out.

"And not entirely true," Lenore complained. "I've been married."

"Three times. We know," chimed in his other two aunts with a roll of their eyes. Which would have set off another argument if their phones hadn't all pinged at once.

"It's him again," muttered Lenore.

"For a guy who was never going to marry, he's awfully pushy about it now," said Lena with a sniff.

"I think it's cute," exclaimed Lacey.

"Oh, please. It's because he's horny." Aunt Lena wagged her finger. "I hear that Tigranov girl won't let him have any until they're married."

"That's because Grandma threatened to geld Dean if he touched her before their union was sanctified," Lacey told them in a theatrical hush that probably everyone heard for a mile around.

All true. Lawrence had to listen to his best friend as he moaned about the lack of nookie.

"I never knew tigers could be such sticklers for propriety," Lenore declared with a shake of her head. "In my day—"

"Woman wore stirrup pants and thought they were sexy." Lena snorted.

"Don't be snickering so hard. You had the same teased hair." An arched brow went with Lenore's rejoinder.

"But I had the good sense to never wear those fluorescent biker shorts," Lena said with a tilt of her chin.

As the newest fight ramped up, Lawrence, being a shit disturber, just had to toss in, "Okay, boomers."

It almost cost him one of his lives.

Luckily, the aunts loved him, and they all made it to the wedding on time and got to see confirmed bachelor Neville Dean Horatio Fitzpatrick get married. His best friend had chosen to bind himself to one woman—gulp—for life.

Despite what the married folks and others said, it gave Lawrence the shudders. He couldn't even manage six days in a relationship. How the heck did forever work? He knew firsthand how the whole dating thing worked; the first date was always the best, sometimes he could squeak a decent second. By the third, it was all downhill.

Best to keep things short and sweet. He planned to be single forever. But that didn't mean he didn't enjoy the company of women.

And weddings were a great place to get laid.

The ceremony was thankfully boring, the grandmother having bribed some bishop or other to officiate. Apparently, it was a prestige thing. It meant standing in place, or kneeling, only rarely sitting, and there was singing. Lots of it.

As best man, Lawrence suffered it all. On a positive note, this time the bride didn't try to kill him. A long story and the main reason why Dean and Natasha got together.

The reception after the wedding provided a massive buffet, a live band, and lots of bodies, a good number of them shimmying and swaying. They couldn't resist a good beat.

Many of them he already knew. Cousin. Cousin.

Second cousin—which still counted as family when it came to extracurricular bedroom activities. His aunts. Dean's aunts. Then there were the ones he knew he shouldn't go near. Daughter of a Russian mobster. Wife. More wives. A few grandmas who smiled at him. The prospects appeared rather slim.

And then she emerged.

Cute as a chipmunk, her hair swept into a ponytail, glasses dark-rimmed and rectangular. Her curves just right. Her humanity on display as she managed to trip over her own feet and go flying.

CHAPTER TWO

The tray almost slipped out of Charlotte's hands as the door to the kitchen swung open requiring she lean out of the way. The tray she carried—with a double layer of bacon-wrapped shrimp and scallops—tilted slightly, but none of the appetizers hit the floor. She managed to straighten herself without mishap and sighed in relief. Disaster averted.

Usually, she stuck to washing dishes because she was known to be clumsy, but they'd been short staffed on the floor, and she fit in the uniform of black slacks and white blouse. Clumsy or not, they wanted her serving food.

The tray seemed easy enough to hold on to, except for the fact it proved more unwieldy than expected. But other people did it all the time. She'd get better with practice. She'd learned all kinds of new skills since she'd left a decent-paying job in a marketing firm to come to Russia. Given she didn't speak the language, her working choices proved limited. Currently, she had two jobs, one to survive, the other to save so she could go back home.

This evening's gig involved a catered meal for an after-wedding reception being held at a hotel featuring some of the most gorgeous people Charlotte had ever seen. Tall, muscular men, athletic women, graceful in a way that only made her ultra-conscious about her own shortcomings, like literally short. By at least a foot on most of them.

If someone called her fun-sized one more time, she might show them the biggest advantage to her height. She'd dropped a few guys in the past for thinking they could get fresh with her.

But what of the older women that had patted her on the head and asked if she shouldn't be in bed? It seemed wrong to hit them, and at the same time, hello! She didn't look that young.

"Are you going to stand there all night? Serve that food," barked Viktor, the guy running the kitchen.

"Yes, chef," she barked. She could do this. *Just don't drop it.* Easy peasy.

Shoulders back, hands gripping the tray tight, with a bump of her hip, Charlotte went out the door and was hit by a wave of noise. The last time she'd gone out, placing fresh baskets of bread on tables, there'd been a few people. A fraction to what had arrived since.

The room overflowed, boisterous with life. The towering guests moved with a grace that slowed her as she hesitated in front of the door. She went from confident to awkward. Her feet tangled, and she pitched forward, the tray held out in front of her. So much food about to be wasted. *"Please don't let this come out of my paycheck."*

She shuttered her gaze for impact, only to jolt slightly as her upper body hit something hard. An arm curled around her waist to steady her, and the tray was plucked from her hands. At least it hadn't crashed.

She cracked open an eye and then blinked them both at the sight of a man balancing her tray in one hand. The stranger knelt, offering his upper thigh as a cushion, while his other arm—the one that stopped her from face-planting—remained around her waist. Holy smokes. The guy had the reflexes of a superhero.

"Superman, I hope," was a deep, rumbled reply. "He always did look good in those tights. But I have to say that Cavill fellow looks even better as the Witcher."

Oh, dear God, he'd heard her say it aloud. Her cheeks heated as she mumbled, "I said thank you."

"In that case, you're welcome." His smile was much too perfect. He was too...just too much.

Charlotte pushed away from her savior and stood. "Thanks for stopping my fall."

He rose to face her, still balancing the tray with only one palm. How did he do that? She doubted she could have held it for one second before it tilted.

"The pleasure is mine." He practically purred.

The flirting was wasted on her. She held out her hands. "I'll take that back now."

"What if I want it?"

"You can't have it. It's for everyone," she stated, fingers wriggling insistently.

"But I don't like to share, and I love to eat." He winked and popped one of the appetizers into his mouth.

"Does that corny line seriously work on anyone?"

Horror engulfed her as she realized she'd yet again spoken aloud. She blamed fatigue. So damned tired. And still at least four more hours to go. She might need to chug some caffeine. And then hopefully not crash until she got home.

"Do you think I'm flirting?" he asked, flirting.

She ignored the charm. "Give me my tray."

"Say please."

She looked at his smirk. The way he tried to manipulate her into getting what he wanted. Not today, Satan. "You want it. Keep it. I'll go get another."

"Wait."

She'd already turned her back on him, and lucky for her, her mishap was seen. While the sous chef harangued her, they found someone to take her spot and put her back on washing dishes. She didn't leave the kitchen for a few hours, didn't have time to breathe hardly as the rush was on. Food was cooked and served in a nonstop chain. Dishes moved rapidly. She scrubbed to keep up, content with the monotonous work, the kind she could do by rote that allowed her to think about her next move.

She almost had enough for a plane ticket back home, and at least three months' rent. Her issue was she didn't have a place to go, and should she even leave? She'd not yet found her brother.

Where are you, Peter? She'd yet to find any trace of him. Just a small apartment that she took over during her search. Five months of futility.

It hurt to contemplate, but even she had to admit it was time for her to give up.

As the evening waned, the party only got livelier.

The music provided a thumping bass that gave her a rhythm she washed to. Even with the rubber gloves, her hands wrinkled from the moisture. Her skin felt dewy, or it might have been sweat. A kitchen wasn't a place to cool off.

Around midnight, they sent her on a meal break. Thirty minutes all to herself, and she knew how she wanted to spend them. Outside and yet not because she smoked. With winter here, she took a moment to slide on her boots, not exactly fashionable but they were warm and waterproof. She tucked her pants inside them and then donned a sweater and jacket. A scarf was the last thing she wound around her head before heading outside, hands bare in her pockets. She'd either managed to lose her gloves since she arrived or someone *borrowed* them.

She exited the kitchen into the alley, anxious to get out of the steam and smells and into the fresh air. First, a run through the cloud of cigarette and weed smoke that hung around the exit. She shook her head when a hand offered her a hit.

No drugs. No booze. No nothing. Some might call her boring. They'd be right. She'd already lived her party years. She never planned on going back.

Escaping the smoke, she found herself basting in a miasma of garbage, the container overflowing with bags and filth. Quite pungent despite the cold. She didn't even want to imagine the stench in summer.

Fresh air remained elusive, but she intended to find it. To give herself a quiet spot to just plain relax. Ducking her chin into the collar of her coat, she strode with purpose in the direction of the street behind the reception building. If she recalled correctly, it was a quiet road, the businesses being closed for the night.

The moment she popped out of the alley, she glanced around. Being not only a woman but also someone far from home, she had to be extra vigilant.

The road was empty in both directions.

Alone at last. The tension in her shoulders eased as she leaned against the cold brick and pulled out her phone, checking for the millionth time for a message from a contact labeled The Pumpkin Eater. A joke between her and her baby brother.

They'd been so close growing up, but then their parents died when they were teens. An aunt took them in, but a scholarship to college took Charlotte away. Peter seemed to be doing all right. He got a chance to play soccer overseas and did so for a few years until he hurt his knee. Even then, he remained on the other continent, claiming he was working on a special project that took him all over Europe and, most recently, Russia.

Seven months since she'd last heard from him. They'd never gone longer than a month before. By the end of the second month, she'd flown over. She'd spent the next five in a fruitless search. She didn't have a single clue to her brother's whereabouts or wellbeing. Not one. She was lonely and tired of eking out an existence. It was time to go home before officials kicked her out.

She'd been granted a six-month work visa, her other job as an English tutor being her official reason for being in Russia. Apparently, people would pay to spend a few hours with someone who could only communicate in

English. A good gig, however, her permit would soon expire. It gave her no choice but to return to America, only she had nothing to go back to.

In her quest, she'd given up her apartment, her life, and had apparently recently lost all her belongings in a fire at the storage unit she'd rented. Insurance money would replace the furniture, but what of the personal effects? She tried not to have a tiny violin moment, but it was hard to not fall into a morass of self-pity.

Woe is me.

The deep voice startled. "You shouldn't be out here by yourself."

Her whole body jolted, and she lifted her head. How had she not heard him sneaking up on her? And what was *he* doing here?

Despite the fact his features remained in shadow, she recognized him. The handsome and arrogant man from the party who'd rescued her tray. "I'm fine." And then because she knew to never encourage a stranger, "I'm surprised you don't need a wheelbarrow to move after taking on that entire tray of food."

The sassy reply chased his brows up his forehead, and he smiled. "After you left, I decided I was being selfish, and so I shared with a few of my friends. You most definitely do not look fine. Is something wrong?"

"How I look is none of your business. Now if you don't mind, I'm on my break. If you need something, I suggest you return to the party." Yes, it emerged kind of rude, and yet at the same time, she didn't like this stranger being with her alone in a place where she couldn't expect any help.

"Implying I'm disturbing you." He uttered a short bark of laughter. "I'm so very sorry, Peanut." His English didn't have any trace of an accent, and his teeth gleamed white from the shadows.

"My name isn't Peanut."

"What is it then? Mine is Lawrence."

She shouldn't encourage him, and yet she found herself saying, "Charlotte."

"The web-weaving type or the kind who prefers Charlie?"

"The kind that is wasting her break talking to you." Apparently, she'd have to be blunt, or he wouldn't leave her alone.

"Can you blame me for wanting to make conversation with a beautiful lady?"

That brought a huge snort. "I've been washing dishes for hours. I'm wearing the most hideous coat and a giant woolly scarf. Hardly pretty. But I am cold. I should get back inside." She shoved away from the wall, only to have him sidestep.

"So soon?"

"I'm not being paid to talk to you. If you'll excuse me." She went to move around him, only he shifted again.

"Perhaps later, after you finish work."

He was one of *those* guys. The kind who didn't understand when a woman wasn't interested.

She pulled a can of mace from her pocket and brandished it. "Back off."

"No need to be so violent."

"Apparently, there is," she muttered as she evil-eyed him the entire time she skirted his body.

"So that's a no for later?"

She felt perfectly justified in the middle finger she shoved over her shoulder. Enough was enough.

She stomped harder as his laughter followed until she turned the corner into the alley. The light in it flickered. *Bzzt. Bzzt.* Someone needed to tighten it.

The flare of a red-tipped cigarette from up ahead was the only sign she wasn't alone. No big deal. The alley was a popular place to smoke. Probably one of the kitchen staff. She'd passed a few on her way out.

The scuff of a shoe on pavement came from behind. That jerk better not be following her. She whirled with the can of mace at the ready and saw two people—a man and a woman—wearing leather and bad intent. Their eye contact and smirks made it clear they stalked her. She just had to get back to the kitchen and she'd be safe.

She whirled, ready to run, only to find a second man standing in front of her.

"Hello, there." He grabbed her by the arm.

"Help!"

CHAPTER THREE

L awrence had been soundly rejected. Bluntly, too. The aunts would have hit the floor laughing.

It stung. Why did she appear so determined to dislike him? He'd done no wrong. It made him feel less than charitable toward her, and yet when he saw the two figures slip into the alley after her, he followed. It might be nothing, and yet the hairs on his body tingled.

"Help!"

He heard her cry out, and all caution fled. He loped into the alley and took in the situation at a glance.

Two—no, make that three—people confronted the waitress he'd been flirting with. They loomed over her petite frame, menacing her with their size and presence.

Oh, like hell. What appeared as bad odds for Charlotte would be sporting fun for him.

"Where is he? We know you've seen him. Tell me where he is, or I'll hurt you," the biggest one threatened in a heavy accent, only to screech as the lady used her can of mace.

That almost had his graceful ass stumbling. She might be human, she might be tiny, but hot damn she was mighty.

"Get your hands off me," she yelled while continuing to spray, only it went from a fine mist to spitting drops. Then nothing.

The red-eyed thug wiped at his eyes. He looked pissed. Shit was about to get ugly real quick. He needed to draw attention away from her.

"Hey, assholes, wrong person. It's me you're looking for." Lawrence waved. Then taunted, "Come and get me."

The thug with streaming eyes snapped something in Russian and squinted in his direction. The conversation resulted in some shrugging. The woman, her long hair plaited down her back, grabbed hold of Charlotte's arm. Peanut's mighty glare did not burn the grip to ash.

Lawrence would need to give her a hand. Pity he couldn't pop a claw. He dropped into a semi-crouch, knowing he couldn't exactly shift, not this publicly. Too many witnesses around. He didn't need his liger to handle three street thugs. He rotated his fists as he bounced on his heels, drawing their eyes. Let them get hypnotized by his movement.

The thugs moved in, splitting apart, thinking they could rush him from opposing directions. He dropped down and kicked, snaring the tallest of the group around the ankle and toppling him. Lawrence was just in time to pop up as the second thug, the one with the beard, dove at him. Had only enough time to place his hands on his chest and propel him away. The fellow hit the wall hard and slumped to the ground, dazed for the moment, but not out of it yet.

The one he'd tripped had recovered and came at him. They hit the ground and grappled, messing up his suit. There went the deposit on that rental. It happened a lot more often than it should.

He managed a head butt that knocked out his attacker, which then left him the bearded guy. It took only a little maneuvering before he had a grip around the man's neck and applied pressure to make him pass out.

Lawrence only eased up when he heard an ominous, "Let him go and come quietly, or she dies."

A quick glance showed the woman, holding Charlotte against her chest. She had at least a foot and probably a hundred pounds on Peanut. She held a knife at Charlotte's throat hard enough to pierce skin and draw a bead of blood.

Ah shit. "Don't you worry, Peanut. I'll get you out of this safe."

"Drop Jarl," the woman demanded in a strong accent.

Now it should be noted Lawrence could technically kill everyone in this alley. A snap of a few necks, even a quick shift into his liger, a few swipes of his claws, and he'd emerge victorious. But Charlotte would probably end up dead.

Some of his friends would say, so what? She didn't belong to the Pride. She wasn't anyone really, and yet he wasn't the kind of guy to let an innocent be killed, not on his account. Besides, he was curious. Who had sent a team of humans to find him?

He'd heard them asking Charlotte where he was. Why her of all people? He'd just met her.

The thugs had probably spotted them together on the street. Meaning the attack was kind of his fault. But who were they?

To find out, he'd have to go with the thugs somewhere a little more private. Getting answers might involve screaming.

"You win." He flung red-eyed Jarl from him and held out his hands. "I'll come nicely, just don't hurt the girl. She has nothing to do with this."

Apparently, he should have included himself in that deal. Jarl had some anger issues and took it out on Lawrence as he tugged a burlap bag over his head—handy how they kept a stash in the trunk—and zip tied his hands behind his back.

Laughable really. He could have snapped those without even trying.

Then they thought to humiliate him by shoving him in the direction of the car, waiting to laugh as he fell. Please. A cat always remained on his feet.

His captors had a conversation in Russian, the only word he recognized being "large." Probably talking about him. Two Russian girls he'd dated had said it often enough.

He heard doors unlock; however, Lawrence was less than impressed when they stuffed him into the trunk while the waitress with the lovely smell got to ride in the back seat!

CHAPTER FOUR

Charlotte sat squished against the door as far as she could get from the not-so-nice guy she'd sprayed in the eyes. Jarl didn't seem too happy with her and now was taking her somewhere with him.

She tried not to panic. Tell that to her racing heart and clammy hands. Not to mention the guilt she felt that the guy who'd come to her rescue got caught in her mess.

This had to be about her brother. What kind of trouble had Peter gotten into this time? Drugs? She'd thought he'd finally gotten clear of them after spending those six months in jail.

Was it stealing? Had he been so stupid again? He'd only gotten off the last time because he'd negotiated a plea deal by giving them a bigger fish.

Whatever the reason, she'd give him an earful when he surfaced. Because Peter would return. Anything else wasn't acceptable.

Although perhaps it was time to worry for herself.

What did they want with her? And why had they taken that other guy? What had he said his name was?

It took her only a moment to remember his purred, *Lawrence.*

He'd come to her rescue and gotten stuffed into a trunk for the effort. A heroic if foolish gesture. Or not so foolish since technically he'd been winning the fight in the alley until she got caught by Mrs. Mean Lady, who really needed to do something about that funky smell.

"Where are you taking me?"

"Quiet," Mrs. Mean Lady snapped from her spot in the front seat.

"You can't just kidnap me," she said, only to have the woman whirl and glare.

"I said quiet."

"Or else," added a much-too-gleeful voice from her left side.

Jarl, with his very red eyes, dropped a heavy hand on her thigh. She pushed it off and huddled against the door, trying to not hyperventilate.

Would they hurt her? Because they certainly appeared determined to terrify her. Technically, they'd not hurt her yet, if she ignored the spot of blood on her neck. But just because they wanted her alive for something didn't make that reason any good.

Their intent became more ominous with every mile that took them out of the city. From bright lights to sketchy dark roads, they drove long enough she managed a fitful nap and woke drooling on the window. As she shifted her body, she realized Jarl had his hand high on her thigh. She flung it off with disgust.

He leered and licked his lips.

She shuddered.

"We're here," Mean Lady said. "Do not try to escape. There is nowhere to go."

For some reason, Charlotte knew this to be the truth. They'd stopped at a decrepit house well outside the city limits. In the dawning light she saw the cleared fields covered in a light layer of snow, the pickets of a fence still standing in some spots. At one time it might have been a farm, but the weathered barn had caved in, and the house with its lopsided appearance and sagging roof looked close to following.

A rough grip around her upper arm dragged her from the car, and Mean Lady marched her up the steps.

She couldn't help gasping, "What do you want from me? Is this about my brother? What's going to happen?"

"Shut up." The heavily accented demand came with a rough shake.

Charlotte cried out in pain then wondered at the creaking that erupted from the trunk. Wait, was the car bouncing?

Mean Lady barked something at the bearded guy, who thumped the trunk with his fist and yelled something in Russian. Probably along the lines of calm down.

How could anyone calm down? This was an epic disaster.

The car stopped shaking, and only then did the bearded guy pop the trunk. Lawrence sat up, looking only slightly disheveled, and drawled, "Thanks for the lovely nap."

"Shut the fuck up." Jarl's eyes were still blood red

and weeping constantly, and this despite the bottle of water he'd poured over them. He looked exhausted and sickly with a huge hint of angry. He shoved past Charlotte in the direction of the house, dug a key out from his pocket, and slotted it into the lock. Because they totally needed to lock the door on a house in the middle of nowhere.

Mean Lady shoved Charlotte in the direction of the open door. If she went inside, that was it. She knew how this ended in the books. They'd probably kill her. Hurt her badly at the very least.

She panicked, and her feet tangled. In moments, her clumsy body pitched.

No one saved her that time, but she did get her hands out quickly enough so only the palms truly felt the pain. Her face had been saved this time. Her glasses, too. She'd been lucky not to lose them. She was pretty nearsighted without. One day, when she could afford it, she'd get that laser surgery and discover what it was like to wake up in the morning and not have to squint at her clock.

Today was not that day.

She was yanked to her feet roughly and shoved in the direction of the door again. She stumbled and did her best not to faceplant a second time. Through her own terror, she heard a rumbling growl.

Did the countryside have wild animals? She cast a fearful glance over her shoulder and, despite the barren, snow-dusted fields, wondered if she'd be safer inside.

The hallway proved as decrepit as the exterior, the wallpaper peeling, the plaster uneven and cracked in a few places where it showed through. She caught a glimpse of a room with a couch, the seat sagging in a huge dip, a few mismatched wooden chairs, a cold fireplace.

The kidnappers were talking in Russian again, meaning she had no idea what was happening. Propelled in the direction of the stairs, Charlotte climbed. Where else would she go?

A door at the far end of a sloping hall boasted a hasp, and a padlock hanging loose. It wasn't hard to guess their destination.

She balked at the doorway. Entering would truly make her a prisoner.

"No. I—"

They didn't listen. The shove sent her reeling over the threshold, tripping over a mattress on the floor. She sat down hard enough she knocked her teeth.

For a few thudding heartbeats, she remained still. During that respite, she took in the hideous room with its peeling flowered wallpaper, illuminated by a bare light bulb hanging from the ceiling. The mattress had a ratty blanket crumpled on it and nothing for a bottom sheet. The stains proved many and varied, the different shades of yellow, brown, and even putrid green had her shoving away from it and sitting in a dusty corner.

More than ever, she wished she'd stayed in the States. No one knew where she was. No one would even think to look for her when she went missing.

Dumb. So freaking dumb.

She had to escape. The door would be locked; she'd heard them click it the moment they had her inside. Which left the window.

Rising, she moved for it, only to find it nailed shut.

"No." She curled her fingers on the ledge and leaned her forehead on the dirty glass. Well and truly screwed.

Click. She whirled as the door suddenly opened again, and Lawrence was thrust inside. Or more like he walked right in. The portal slammed shut and was locked. But at least she wasn't alone.

Unlike her, Lawrence didn't appear agitated at all. He flashed a smile. "Hey, Peanut. You look a little frazzled. Did someone hurt you?"

"Not yet, but it's coming." She wrung her hands. "We are so screwed."

"Why would you think that?"

She gaped at him for a second. "Are you not paying attention? We've been kidnapped. Locked in a room. We'll probably be tortured. Or killed. Or worse."

"There's something worse?" he asked, arching a brow.

"I'm a woman, of course there's worse. And given you're a pretty boy, you should be worried, too."

His jaw dropped, and then his shoulders shook as he laughed. "That will never happen."

"As if you'll have a choice. There's too many of them."

"Bah. Three is nothing. This time, I'll make sure you're safely out of reach and then *rawr*." He faked a roar that had Charlotte rolling her eyes.

"Pretending you're a ferocious lion isn't going to help us. Those bad people have knives and guns. They're dangerous."

"Don't you worry about them, Peanut."

"Don't worry? Have you lost your mind? We are locked in a room in the middle of nowhere with murderers. We are so screwed," she moaned. Not to mention, if they were killers, then that meant there was little chance of Peter still being alive. Any hope left in her shriveled and died.

"Have a little faith, Peanut."

"My name isn't Peanut."

"And you don't like Charlie."

"What's wrong with Charlotte?"

"I'd say our shared experience has moved us past formal names. You may call me Law."

"I am going to call you Annoying if you don't stop. Now is not the time to be flirting or playing your stupid games," she huffed

"First off, it's always a good time to flirt, and second, this isn't a game." He winked. "It's called banter and is meant to calm your nerves."

"My nerves are fine."

"Says the woman shaking like a leaf."

She was? Charlotte glanced down and saw her body trembling. Only for a second, then she was engulfed in a hug.

The first word out of her mouth was, "Hey," but before the rest could slip, the warmth penetrated her chill, the tension in her shoulders eased a slight bit, and somehow she felt less anxious overall. She didn't remember a high feeling so good. So right.

He broke the spell, not by the hand stroking down her back, but his murmured, "That's my Peanut.

"I am not your anything." She moved away from him.

"This is not the time to be screwing around. We are in so much trouble." It surprised her that Lawrence had not asked why yet. How to explain that her brother didn't always follow the laws?

"We'll be fine."

"Your optimism might be misplaced."

"You forgot to add in absolute arrogance because I'm too pretty to die young." He winked. "And so are you."

He thought her pretty? *No. Don't get distracted.* She shook her head. "I don't know how you can be optimistic."

"Guess you'll just have to trust me."

Trust him? She'd just met him, and he'd yet to make a good impression outside of the whole trying-to-save-her thing.

With not much to do other than be nervous, time passed slowly. To his credit, Lawrence tried to ease the situation with witty talk. Most of it went in one ear and out the other. She was turned inward, trying to think of a way out, and thus not paying much attention.

Lunch arrived, bread and cheese with some rusty-looking water. At least they wouldn't be starved. Or she wouldn't. Lawrence took one sniff and turned up his nose.

"I am not eating that crap."

"More for me, then." She refused to cajole him into having some. He was a grown man. Let him starve if he was going to be picky. She tucked it away for later in case their next meal didn't come as promptly.

Just after dusk there was the sound of a car approaching. A peek from the window showed nothing, but she could hear voices. New ones, at least three, perhaps more, along with doors slamming.

Then silence except for the thump of feet on the stairs and the creak as they came down the hall.

Lawrence abandoned his spot by the window and stood in front of the door a second before it slammed open. The biggest of the thugs filled the opening. With that beard and expression, he needed only an eye patch to make the perfect pirate. He crooked a finger in her direction.

Gulp. The time had come. Hopefully it wouldn't hurt.

As she went to step around Lawrence, he put out his arm to stop her. "I appreciate your support, Peanut, but I'll handle this." And then he embarrassed her with his drawled, "Would it kill you to knock? What if I'd been getting busy with the lady?"

CHAPTER FIVE

Lawrence rightly deserved her weak punch to the kidney. His words were crude and rife with innuendo, but for a good reason. Best to lay a claim on the woman now before this perv thought he could put his hands on her. Any thoughts they had about touching his Peanut ended now.

He stood in front of Brownbeard, and added, "Do you have a tie or a sock we can use to signal when you can visit?"

"What are you doing?" she hissed.

"Staking a claim so they know you're taken," he muttered back. "I suggest you play along." Even if the guy in front of him apparently didn't understand a word.

Brownbeard nattered something in Russian. It brought the leering one with his red eyes to join the party.

"What is problem now?" Jarl asked rather testily, shoving Brownbeard to the side.

"I was just explaining to your friend that it's not cool to be a cockblocker."

"Oh!" Charlotte's exclamation was a precursor to her jab against his lower back.

"Your mouth, it moves too much," Jarl complained.

"I'll have you know my mouth is one of my most valuable body parts. I've been told I'm orally gifted, and not just in the bedroom." He winked, not actually flirting with the thug but trying to throw him off balance. It worked.

Jarl reeled, his thin features contorting. "Not interested."

"Then why have you taken me?" Lawrence boldly asked in hopes of an answer. Was this another case of a crazy ex-girlfriend?

"The boss speak with you."

"What boss?"

"The big boss. Don't play stupid. You know what you have done," Jarl stated.

Lawrence shook his head. "Dude, I've done a lot of things. You'll have to be more specific. The only thing I know for sure is whatever has you pissed, she's not a part of. Let her go."

"Quietness, now, I command."

"Did you study under the great green master? Or should I say, under his eye study you did."

Jarl growled. "Come. Now!" Jarl and Bearded stepped to either side of the door and waited for him.

Only as they moved to close the portal did he realize Charlotte wasn't coming. "What are you planning to do with her?"

"Whatever I like." Jarl guffawed and totally deserved the punch to the face that cracked his nose. Only once the annoying man started gushing blood and screaming did Lawrence tuck his hands behind his back. Brownbeard stared at Jarl then Lawrence.

Lawrence shrugged. "He shouldn't talk smack about a lady."

"Kind of ironic you'd say that," she muttered.

Actually, more like hypocritical. She didn't know him well enough to see how he used his words to his advantage. The right phrase could knock the staunchest person off balance. Bullies especially hated being mocked. It made them rash. Look at Jarl, who came swinging, only to get knocked down.

At Brownbeard's heavy sigh, Lawrence made a gesture of, what do you expect? When Jarl would have come for a third smackdown, Brownbeard stood in his way and barked something in Russian, to which Jarl replied. Judging by the tone—sulky with a chance of repercussion—Jarl would wait to exact his revenge.

Bring it. Next time, Lawrence wouldn't just wreck his face.

Jarl shut the door leaving Charlotte alone inside. They flanked Lawrence down the hall. The stairs creaked ominously with the three big men on them at once, but they survived and made it to the main floor, which was lit with a variety of naked bulbs and a few lamps, some of which flickered. Old place like this, it was surprising it still had power.

The dance of shadows might have proved more ominous and impressive to someone else. The granite expressions of the two new men were boring. The guns the guards bore might be a problem, but only if they managed to get them out and aimed in time. He didn't plan to move slowly when he acted.

A woman, still wearing her outer garment, sat on someone's spread coat on the sagging couch. Heavy mascara lined her eyes. Must be the boss.

"You're bigger than I was led to expect," she declared.

"All over, baby." Said with a wink.

Her lips, heavily rouged, pursed. "Tell us where it is."

"Where what is?"

"Do not play stupid. I am aware of the reason you came to Russia."

"My best friend's wedding wasn't exactly a secret."

"What wedding? Do not change the subject. Did you find it?" She leaned forward.

His turn to appear perplexed. "Find what? I don't know what you're talking about."

"You lie." She slammed her carved wooden cane on the floor and almost lunged from the couch. "We know you were hot on its trail. You said so in the letter we intercepted."

The story twisted a bit more and still had nothing to do with him, but he was intrigued. A feline trait. "What makes you think I want to give it to you?" Perhaps playing along would get her to reveal more.

"Hand it over, or we will hurt her."

"What makes you think I care what happens to Charlotte?" He did, but admitting that meant examining why. He'd met her only the night before. She hated him. And yet he had this urge to protect her. Then again, he'd protect anyone in the Pride who got caught in a bad situation.

A thinly plucked brow arched. "Are you saying you don't care?" She smiled. A wicked thing more ominous than a cat crossing someone's path. "Jarl will be happy to hear that. He's always had a thing for American girls."

The implication drew a growl from him. "Leave her alone."

"If you want to keep her safe, then you will give me what I want."

First impulse involved telling her to shove her demands somewhere moist. The rash choice. There were quite a few guards in this room, not to mention others that might get to Charlotte before he could. He needed to even the odds. Never attack at a disadvantage unless your life truly depended on it. He looked for a way to stall. "What if I don't have it yet?"

"Then you will tell us where it is."

"And if I say no? Are you going to take me to the basement and torture me?" he offered. That would probably thin out the guards around him. Not many people could handle the screaming and the blood.

"Torture is too messy and inconclusive." Boss Lady wrinkled her nose before giving a shark grin. "In these modern times, we use drugs. Lucky you, I've got a new version of a truth serum to try." She snapped her fingers, and there was movement behind him.

As he turned to see a big dude reaching out, he raised his arms to block and missed the guy sneaking in behind.

The pinprick in his arm was like the smallest of stings. There and gone, not even worth his attention.

But perhaps he should have minded it because his senses clouded almost instantly. His vision filmed over, and when next he regained consciousness, it was to find himself in a strange cabin in bed with a woman.

A human and—judging by the scent on her and by the marks at her neck—his mate.

CHAPTER SIX

"Who are you?" Lawrence woke as suddenly as he'd passed out and eyeballed Charlotte as if he'd never seen her before.

Kind of ballsy given his weight still pinned her to the bed.

The fact he asked made her a tad terse. "Don't you dare pretend you don't remember."

"Everything is fuzzy." He grimaced and shut his eyes, his brow furrowing. "Did I drink too much?"

"You tell me, and while you're figuring it out, how about you let me loose. Not everyone likes being squished like a bug," she snapped, still miffed he'd forgotten her. So much for his outrageous flirting. She was just another nameless woman to him.

"Can't we keep cuddling a while longer?" he asked.

She wouldn't soften. Not after everything he'd done. "No." She heaved in a deep breath as he rolled off of her.

In an odd twist, she kind of missed the weight. Despite the fact it trapped her, it also reassured. She'd been so terrified back at that abandoned farmhouse, and then he'd come to her rescue. He'd kicked open the door to her prison as if they were in some action movie featuring a big, blond berserker of a Viking warrior. He'd grabbed her attacker and tossed him across the room, his features more feral beast than man. Surely a trick of the light and exaggerated by her frazzled nerves.

Only, he'd acted wild, too.

Her hand went to her neck, sticky with dried blood, and yet no pain. "Sorry doesn't quite cut it."

His gaze tracked the movement of her fingers. He swallowed hard, and his voice rose an octave as he asked, "What happened? Last thing I remember...I..." His brow turned into a mess of furrows. "I don't remember anything after the needle."

"They drugged you?" That would explain a lot.

"Yeah, with something that was supposed to make me spill my guts, but I guess I had a bad reaction and it put me into a comatose state."

"That would imply you were incapable of acting. I assure you, you were anything but asleep." He'd appeared even more alive than usual. Thrumming with energy.

"What happened?"

Because he obviously didn't remember, she told him, reliving her rescue for the umpteenth time and still unable to make sense of it. "After you left, the guy I maced paid me a visit."

The door to the room creaked open slowly, and Jarl smiled at her from the doorway. He said something in Russian.

She shook her head. "I don't understand."

Jarl stepped into the room and shut the door. The cruel smile tugging his lips widened. "Take off your clothes."

Her head shook wildly as she barked a sharp, "No."

"Do it. Or else."

How could his "or else" be worse than what would happen if she obeyed? His intent was obviously evil.

Her chin lifted. "I am not doing anything for you. Release me." A bold demand that got the expected laughter.

"You want to fight? Let us fight." He beckoned, eager for it, knowing she was screwed. A can of mace and a well-aimed knee was about the extent of her self-defense abilities. "Take off your clothes, or I'll do it for you." The switchblade emerged from a pocket, and her mouth went dry.

If she fought, he might cut her. If she didn't... He might still cut her. A no-win situation, so what would be the deciding factor? Courage or cowardice?

Charlotte screamed and ran for him, her quickly formulated plan being to startle him enough she could dart past him. Maybe make it to the hall and the stairs.

Then what? She'd figure it out if she— Oomph.

She slammed into his midsection, and he belched a huge grunt. But he didn't budge. He recovered quickly and shoved her from him, brandishing the knife before him, muttering a stream of Russian curses, some of which she understood. They were the first words she'd picked up when she relocated.

Jarl advanced on her, no longer laughing or smiling.

She might have made things worse. She retreated, but she didn't have far to go. Her back hit the wall and halted her escape.

He stopped right in front of her. His fetid breath washed over her face as he leaned down and whispered in Russian. Probably something violent and obscene.

She closed her eyes as the tip of the knife came to rest on her blouse, right by the first button.

Then the door slammed open. Hard enough that it hit the wall with a bang and bounced.

In stalked Lawrence, his eyes almost glowing in his rage, his lip pulled back in a snarl. He appeared utterly ferocious and acted completely unafraid as he went after Jarl and his knife.

There wasn't actually any competition. Lawrence picked Jarl up as if he weighed nothing and tossed him. The thug thudded into the wall and slumped.

Lawrence wasn't done. He grabbed Jarl by the shirt and hauled him over to the nailed window. He shoved the man through it, the glass shattering and falling with the body.

She gaped. "You threw him out a window."

"He deserved it," Lawrence growled as he turned to her, heaving, seething with rage. It was terrifying and captivating all at once. He held out his hand. "Come." His voice sounded different, lower and gruffer than usual. Scary, too.

"What's wrong with you?"

"Nothing. We leave. Now."

"Out there?" In the darkness and cold? She grabbed the coat she'd shed and quickly put it over her sweater.

She'd lost her scarf but still had her boots while Lawrence remained in his suit, now torn and stained with— Was that blood?

She took a step back. How had he escaped and come to her rescue?

He waited by the window, hand outstretched. Did it matter how he'd gotten to her? He was the good guy. Self-defense wasn't a crime, and he wanted to help her escape.

She placed her hand in his, and he drew her against his body, the heat radiating from it welcome considering her inner chill. A peek out the window showed a sad-looking porch roof, the shingles buckling and peeling. On the ground, Jarl rolled and groaned.

"Quickly," said Lawrence. He slid out the window first, proving it large enough, and stood on the roof. It didn't collapse under his weight. He once more held out his hand.

Being careful of the glass in the frame, she stepped out, fingers gripping his, hoping her feet wouldn't slide out on the warped and sloped roof. A sharp yell drew her gaze over her shoulder to see Mean Lady had entered the room.

"They know we're escaping," she exclaimed, rather unnecessarily.

Rather than reply, Lawrence released her hand and quick-stepped to the edge of the porch awning. He didn't hesitate or even look down, just leaped.

She remained frozen for a second after his hissed, "Are you coming?"

Before she could move, she was grabbed. Mean Lady had acted quickly and had a hold. Startled, Charlotte reeled away and managed to break free.

Which set her off balance. She fell on her ass and slid.

Oh shoot—

A thought that started during her plummet but ended as she was caught by brawny arms.

She blinked. "Am I alive?"

The grin on Lawrence's face was much too happy for the situation. "As if there was any doubt."

Someone yelled, setting off the alarm at their escape. There were on the far side of the house from the front door, in partial shadow, and yet it wouldn't be long before they were spotted.

"Let's go."

Lawrence laced his fingers in hers and pulled her into a run, kicking at Jarl as they passed, sending him back to the ground.

Charlotte tried. She really did, but she couldn't keep up with his pace. Her feet had no rhythm; she kept stumbling and tripping. When he abruptly stopped, she thought for sure he'd yell at her for being so clumsy and slow.

Instead, he tossed her over his shoulder and took off running again, so fast their previous pace was like walking in comparison. The night air bit coldly, and his shoulder dug into her stomach. The lightly falling snow didn't improve the situation, but it apparently muddled the trail because he sprinted across the fields for the woods and made it within the boundaries. The yelling faded, as did all light, but he didn't stop.

Lawrence kept running, jostling her as she clung to him, face buried against his back. It lasted minutes. Hours. She couldn't have said, only that she was sore when he finally slowed. He didn't set her down even when they reached a ramshackle cabin. He didn't knock, simply booted open the door, which was pretty brave given she expected it to fall over with the slightest blow.

The inside proved more solid than expected and yet decrepit, with everything covered in a thick layer of dust. The cobwebs had cobwebs. There were mice droppings and other hard lumps of poop that had solidified over time. Basic furniture filled the space from a table with a hanging curtain and a crusted basin sitting on top of it to the pair of stools, round disks from a tree trunk on wooden legs. The bed consisted of a pile of abandoned blankets that puffed dirt and probably lung disease when he tossed her onto it.

She coughed and gasped, struggled to escape the surely vermin-infested bedding, only to find herself pinned by Lawrence.

"What are you doing?"

"Sleeping," was his grumbled reply.

"We can't sleep. What if those people come after us?"

"They won't. And it's not them you need to worry about." Rather than explain what that meant, he nuzzled her and growled. Like literally and it was rumbly enough to vibrate her skin.

She could have sworn he turned angry. "What's wrong?"

"I can still smell him on you."

She assumed he meant Jarl. "Don't worry. I'm sure it won't be long before that's replaced by whatever dead and pee-covered aroma permeates this place."

He rubbed his cheek on hers. "I want you to wear my scent."

"That's weird."

"Indeed it is given I've never wanted to do that before." He lifted his head enough he could gaze at her. "There's something different about you, Peanut."

"Is that a bad thing?"

His lips quirked. "I don't know yet. After all, we've only known each other a day."

"Not even." And what a tumultuous time so far.

"I'm tired." He rested his forehead against hers.

"Shouldn't one of us keep watch?"

"I won't let anything harm you." The words flashed hotly over her lips, which parted, as if anticipating a kiss. Only he returned to nuzzling her neck, whispering against her skin, "Why do you smell so good?"

Why did he feel so good? Tingles raced throughout her body. She couldn't help but subtly writhe as his mouth dragged over her neck.

She should push him away.

She deserved this. After all she'd almost died.

She enjoyed it until he bit her.

"What the hell?" she yelled.

"Mine," was his guttural reply.

"And then you started snoring like a freight train." She concluded the story with no mention of how she'd spent a good while after aching between her legs, calling herself all kinds of dumb.

"I do not snore," Lawrence protested.

"Yeah. You do. Loudly. And you weigh a ton."

"Do not." Hotly exclaimed. "I am in excellent shape."

"Never said you weren't. Everyone knows muscle is heavy. I can even testify about it since I was the one squished under you for hours. Maybe even days. You're lucky I didn't have to pee!"

"I was drugged," was his sulky reply.

"Is that the excuse you're going to use to explain why you went all vampire and bit me?"

"Excuse me but I am not a blood-sucking vampire. Wait, I didn't suck your blood, did I?" He sounded hesitant.

"No, but you broke skin. See." She tilted her head to show him her neck.

He appeared shocked. "I cannot believe I did that."

"You did."

He closed his eyes, and his head rolled back. "This isn't good."

"Ya think?" She remained on the bed for the moment, wondering if they'd missed an entire day given how dark it was inside the cabin. Colder now, too. Struggling to sit, she drew her knees to her chest and hugged them.

"It's probably too late to reverse it," he mumbled.

A dumb observation and an odd way of phrasing it. Wait... Was he implying he might have some kind of sickness? Like rabies or something? Wasn't that the bad thing that could happen from bites, or did that apply only to wild animals? Did they have a shot to fix what he'd done?

He reached out to touch, but she flinched. "Oh no

you don't. Last thing I need is your dirty fingers introducing even more bacteria into the wound."

"It won't get infected."

"You can't know that for sure. I need medical attention."

"You'll be fine," he grumbled. He rubbed a hand through his hair. "I don't suppose you happen to know where we are."

She shook her head. "Nope."

"Have a phone?" he asked rather hopefully.

"They took them, and we escaped without getting them back."

"That's unfortunate."

"Unfortunate?" she screeched. "We're lost in the Russian wilderness with killers after us, no food, no car, nothing. We're fucked." She didn't often resort to strong cussing, but these weren't ordinary times.

"You are super cute when you're mad."

"That is the most chauvinistic thing you've said thus far."

"How is telling you you're cute bad?"

"Because."

"And that's where we're different. I'd love to know how handsome I look when I'm angry."

"Less handsome and more like a beast."

His expression turned sober. "You say that like it's a bad thing."

"Because it is. You looked like someone else. It was kind of spooky." Hot too, but she wasn't about to mention that part out loud.

"This is awkward." He grimaced and paced the tight space.

"Shouldn't we be concentrating on finding our way back to civilization instead of worrying about the fact you have a beasty angry face?"

"We are not going anywhere. Given the amount of time we've been gone, it won't be long before someone comes to find us."

Her mouth rounded. "What? Then we need to leave." She didn't want to imagine what would happen if Jarl and the others caught them again.

"Don't panic. The people I'm talking about won't hurt you. Physically at any rate. But they are quite good at embarrassing. Given it's been more than a day since they've been in contact with me, they'll be starting their search soon." He went to the door that had swung closed but barely.

"So we just need to wait for your friends to find us? How? No one knows where we are."

"That won't stop them." He shoved his head outside for a moment before declaring, "About two o'clock in the afternoon. If they're on the ball, then I figure we won't see them until this evening at the earliest. More likely tomorrow. Maybe even the day after if the snow doesn't stop."

"Snow?" She scrambled from the bed, feeling the chill even more than before. Apparently, he'd done her a favor by mauling her in his sleep. She'd not realized just how cold and uninsulated the cottage was. "We should get out of here. Why are we waiting for your friends?"

"Because you're cold and exhausted," he pointed out. "And so am I."

He had a point. He'd carried her for hours, longer than she would have lasted. Still...She hugged herself, as the cold felt more pronounced now that she wasn't draped over him.

"Let's see if I can get a fire going."

"By what? Lighting up the place? It might be an improvement," was her dry remark.

"How about we use the fireplace instead." He gestured to a hole in the wall lined with rocks and dark with soot.

"Can you really get a fire going?" At the possibly of heat, her expression brightened.

"Yes, but here's hoping the chimney is clear." He crouched down and peeked up the chute. "I see a bit of debris, but there is daylight. Hand me the broom."

She opened her mouth to ask what broom when she saw it by the door. Rather than argue that he was ordering her around, she handed it over.

Lawrence shoved it up the chimney, and debris fell. Leaves and branches, other stuff that might be the detritus of a nest.

"That should do it. And good news, this will give us some quick flare. But we'll need wood to keep it going." He glanced around, and before he could ask, she'd grabbed a log from the rough crate by the door.

"Will this work?"

"Yes, but I'll need to find more, or we won't make it through the night."

There was an old lighter sitting on the hearth that

sparked when he struck it. Unfortunately, it didn't do much more than that.

Rather than declare defeat, he pried apart the lighter and used a loose stone from the fireplace to strike what had to be the flint, sparking it over and over into the dried leaves that had fallen. It took a patience she wouldn't have managed herself until it finally caught, a tiny flame with its even bigger curl of smoke.

It grew quickly, licking at the wood, soon crackling as it fed hungrily. She couldn't help but draw close, holding out her hands to the heat. "Oh, that's nice."

"Enjoy it while you can. Given how dry that wood is, it won't last long." He stood and headed for the door.

"Where are you going?"

He cast her a glance over his shoulder as he opened the door and let in a swirl of cold air. "I'm going to see what I can forage."

"What about me?"

"I wouldn't recommend going out of sight of the shack." He left without waiting for a reply.

Left her shivering and suddenly very afraid again. A feeling exacerbated as she peeked outside and saw the gray skies dropping fluffy snowflakes. Already an inch on the ground and falling fast, which had the benefit of quickly hiding his tracks. A gust swirled flakes into her face, and she recoiled, slamming the door shut. It didn't remove all the chill but did block the windy draft. Meanwhile the fire crackled in the fireplace, already throwing out warmth to chase the chill. She wanted to snuggle close to it.

Glancing around, she didn't see many options to get

comfortable. The blankets on the bed were crusty. The mattress would probably fall apart if she tried to drag it close. Under the table with the bowl sink, dishes and pots sat precariously stacked on a shelf.

There was a cabinet still upright on another wall. Three open shelves at the top with more clutter but a closed door shuttered the bottom.

It took a mighty heavy to get it open, the latch on it grimed with age, but inside she found treasure. A pillow and a sleeping bag, plus a patchwork blanket. Musty smelling but protected from the mice and other occupants over the years. She even found some unopened cans. The labels fell off when she grabbed them. Probably expired, but given how her tummy growled, so long as the contents didn't show signs of fuzz or movement when she opened the can, she would have to take a chance.

But not yet. Not in the filth around her.

The broom he'd used for the chimney leaned close by. The stiff bristles snapped off in a few places as she swept the dirt away from the area in front of the hearth. Foolish, as if cleaning would help. Still, she felt better once she'd cleared a spot. Only then did she unzip the sleeping bag and lay it out in front of the fire. The pillow acted as a cushion for her butt. The blanket remained folded for the moment, as the fire had warmed the hut considerably.

It made the brutal blast of cold air all the more startling when the door suddenly opened. Lawrence stood framed in it for a moment, seemingly undaunted by the storm.

"I found the old woodpile."

"Looks like you found the storm too." Snow draped him head to foot, frosting his hair and eyebrows, even clinging to parts of his jaw.

"There's already a few inches on the ground. I predict a few more at the very least before this system moves on. I'm going to get more wood." He dumped an armful into the bin by the door. He made two more trips, filling that box and then piling some beside it.

"Expecting us to get snowed in for a while?" she asked.

"This storm might last hours, or it could be days. Best be prepared."

Days? Before panic could truly set in, he'd disappeared back into the storm. She tidied some more, finding a pot with a handle that fit on the hook inside the hearth. She melted snow in it and rinsed it out three times, along with a pair of tin mugs she found, before letting the snow in it melt and boil, making it safe for drinking.

She hoped.

She poured it into the cleaned mugs then melted more snow and, using a corner of the sweater she'd removed, dampened it and washed her face. Then hands. Hesitating, she finally dabbed at her neck. The bite didn't hurt. Perhaps it wouldn't get infected.

More time passed, and no Lawrence. The storm outside intensified, the wind whistling and at times shaking the cabin. Yet very few drafts made it inside, and not a single flake of snow.

A good shelter. If only it came fully stocked with a pantry.

Time to check out the mystery cans. She rummaged in the rustic kitchen and found a thing that had to be an opener. When she couldn't figure out how to use it, she resorted to drinking more water to quell the hunger pains in her belly.

When Lawrence finally returned, she almost burst into tears of happiness.

I'm not alone.

When she realized she wanted to run to him like some weakling, she instead barked, "And where have you been?"

"Getting us dinner, Peanut. Ever had roasted squirrel?"

CHAPTER SEVEN

C harlotte blanched as he held up his find. Perhaps he should have skinned it and made it look more store bought before bringing it in.

"What is that? Rat?" she asked.

"Squirrel. Tasty when smoked. I don't suppose you found some salt and pepper."

"You brought back road kill?"

"Snare, actually. And is that a no on the seasoning?"

She'd been busy while he was gone. He took in the tidied nature of the cabin, the nest she'd built in front of the fire.

She pointed. "Tons of salt, a shaker of solid pepper, which is probably no good, and something that could be either oregano or weed."

"No one leaves their weed behind." He winked as he entered and shut the door firmly against the storm.

He'd not meant to be outside so long; however, he'd wanted to scout and ensure they were as remote as he believed. In his mad dash while drugged, he'd taken them deep into the forest. Climbing a tree had only shown more trees as far as he could see. Which admittedly wasn't as far as he liked with the impending storm.

He searched for tracks and laid snares for animals. Not everything hibernated all winter long. He tossed his furry catch onto the cleared counter and emptied his pockets of the nuts he'd also found, hidden in the bole of a tree.

"Can we eat those?" She showed interest and grabbed one, turning it in her fingers.

It shouldn't have fascinated him to watch, yet as with everything else about Charlotte, he couldn't help himself. The effect must have been amplified while he was drugged. That would explain why he'd marked her as his mate. Fate, knowing he wouldn't go willingly, had arranged for him to be in a weak spot and swooped in to screw him.

He was mated.

Shackled.

Screwed.

There had to be a way to nullify what he'd done. Charlotte didn't know what he was. Hadn't consented. Probably never would, given she didn't seem to like him most of the time. Whereas he was finding he liked her all too much.

"Earth to abominable snow guy, how do we eat them?" She shook the nut at him, snapping him out of his contemplation.

"We need to roast those before they'll be edible."

"How?" She didn't question his knowledge, but she

did insist on washing the dusty pan they located, and then she listened as he explained how to cook them.

It was only as he dressed his catch that she asked, "How do you know how to do all this? You don't look like the survivalist type."

"What type do I look like?" he asked as he turned from hacking with the dullest knife in existence.

"Not the outdoorsy kind."

"Because I am wearing a nice suit?" He gestured to his now grimy attire. "This was for the wedding and reception."

"What do you usually wear then?"

"Jeans and tees if I'm going out. Track pants the rest of time, when I'm not naked."

Her nose actually wrinkled. "Ew. I didn't need to know that."

He ogled her for a second. "I don't believe I've ever had a woman say that to me before."

"Never told you how conceited you are and how gross you speak?" She arched a brow. "Not everyone you meet is gonna wanna see your junk."

"Just breaking my heart. Crushing my ego."

"I highly doubt that," she said with a snort as she shook the pan and rattled the nuts around atop a rusted rack he'd fitted inside the hearth. "How do we know when these are ready?"

"When you can't stand waiting any longer, so you grab a really hot one, burn yourself trying to crack it, and pop that hot nut in your mouth for a hopefully satisfying crunch."

"Spoken by the voice of experience," she stated, giving the pan yet another wiggle.

"I'm a man of many faces. Spend time with me, and you might see a few of them." No need to tell her about the fact that she'd be the first woman, other than a family member, that he allowed to get close enough to see past the tomcat exterior.

"Guess I won't have a choice. We're going to be stuck here until the morning at least, aren't we? Maybe even longer." Her lips turned down.

"Some women would be delighted at a chance for alone time with me."

She pursed her lips. "I'm not most women."

The thing he liked most about her. "Who are you, Peanut? What secrets are you hiding inside that head of yours?"

"If they're secret, then I'm not going to tell you."

"A woman of mystery," he said as he headed for the door and tossed the unwanted parts of the squirrel outside.

"Hardly. You said something earlier. About your friends finding us."

"I don't know if I'd call them friends." He grimaced. "But if there's one thing I am sure of, there is nowhere on this earth they won't come looking for me."

"But how? Even if they had dogs to trace our scent from that house, the snow would have covered the tracks."

"Let's just say they have other ways." The chip they'd put in him after that kidnapping would show up as a ping on a passing satellite at one point. Once the storm passed, they'd be able to pick up his signal.

"Take it from me, it's not easy finding people who are lost." Her shoulders drooped.

The statement indicated a story, but he didn't prod. Mostly because he didn't think she was ready to relate it yet.

He watched her hesitating to grab a hot nut from the pan she'd placed on the hearth. Her tongue poked from her lips. Her glasses sat low on her nose. A miracle she'd held on to them.

"I'm surprised you still have those." He indicated the frames.

"As a person who has lost or broken a few pairs, the first thing I do in an emergency is get them somewhere safe. I tucked them in my pocket before climbing out of the window."

"Smart and beautiful."

"Still not doing the flirting thing," she reminded.

Even rebuffing him, she was so damned cute.

And his.

The marks were on the other side of her neck, and yet he sensed them. How could he feel them? Why was he so drawn to her? Did the drugs still course through his system? Or had it finally happened? That dreaded thing that seemed to afflict personally reasonable people and turn them into couples?

Look at his best friend, Dean, who'd just married. Volunteered to be tied down by a ball and chain. The guy had never looked happier.

If a confirmed bachelor like Dean could find someone, maybe it wasn't farfetched that Lawrence could too. But was Charlotte the one?

He crouched beside her and flipped the pan, pouring the scorching nuts onto the sleeping bag.

"What are you doing?" she squeaked, jerking away from the piping-hot shells.

"Cooking our dinner." He dumped the seasoned meat into the pan. There was a satisfying sizzle. He returned the pan to the hearth, shoved in far enough to cook.

"How do we eat them?" she asked, having recovered from her freak-out. She leaned forward and made sure she didn't touch the nuts she pointed to.

"Crack them open." He grabbed and pinched one hard enough it split. He handed her the treat inside.

It was three bites before she caught on. She held the nut between two fingers and eyed him. "Aren't you having some?"

"I'm fine."

"Are you, or are these poisoned?" She suddenly held the nut away from her as if it might attack.

He snorted. "Are you always this paranoid?" Only to immediately apologize. His aunts had taught him women experienced a different reality than men. "No, they're not poisoned. I didn't eat any because you are hungry."

"I am, but you need food, too," she insisted.

"Go ahead. I can wait. Dinner is coming." He pointed to the pan.

"Exactly. Which means I won't be greedy. Eat."

To his surprise—and pleasure—she shoved the nut at

his lips. He took it and crunched, his gaze locked with hers. "Thank you."

Her lashes dropped along with her head. "Let me try and open the next one." She sought a nut and squeezed it. It didn't crack. She squished it and strained. Growled in annoyance.

Lawrence didn't smile, but he did snare a pair of nuts. *Crunch.* He opened his hand. "They're kind of tough."

"I can do this," she insisted. She rose, and since she was on some kind of mission, he ate the two nuts.

It didn't take her long to find what she wanted, a meat mallet, the handiest tool to have in the wilderness for tenderizing meat and whacking shit. She lightly tapped a nut. When it didn't crack, she pulverized it.

They both stared at the remains, shell and nut mixing together. "I think that one was bad," she declared.

"Most definitely," he said without hinting at his humor.

The next nut she smashed survived mostly intact, and he let her open all the nuts. They shared them, and when they were done, he swept up the shavings and tossed them into the fire, causing the flames to leap.

The hut remained surprisingly weatherproof. They could hear the whistle of the storm outside, and there were small drafts, but the fireplace chased the chill. They were safe from the snow, and—

"Should we turn it?"

"What?" He startled and took a moment to grasp what she meant. "The meat. Yes." Still somewhat in a bemused state, he snared the pan and hissed at the heat of the handle.

"You might want to use this." She grabbed the makeshift potholder from the floor where it had fallen unnoticed. He blamed her for the distraction.

He reached for it, only to have her grab his hand.

"You're hurt."

"Barely. I don't feel a thing." Not entirely true, his hand did throb, but he knew it wouldn't last long. Shifters healed at a quicker rate. Especially true in some hybrids.

He slid the glove on and pulled the pan close enough that he could roll the meat. It sizzled as it hit the hot metal. He shoved it back for some more cooking. "It will be awhile yet."

"If you're hungry now, I found some cans." She gestured.

"What do we have?" He held one up. "Some kind of green vegetable."

"Sounds delicious?" Her nose scrunched at her query.

The corner of his lip tugged. "That is more optimistic than this image deserves. What do you say we find out?"

"There's a weird can opener." She located the tool, and Lawrence showed her how to peel metal with it.

The moment he pierced that seal, the smell hit them. Hard.

"Oh god, that's awful," she exclaimed. "It must have gone bad."

He peered at the contents. "I don't know. Seems like

it matches the picture. He held it tilted in her direction to show off the green lumps.

"I can't eat that." She put a hand over her mouth.

"Me either." Nor did he want to smell it a minute longer. Opening the door for only the barest of seconds, he tossed it as far as he could into the storm. Something would find it and not be as picky about eating.

The next can held a soup.

"Think it's any good?" she asked dubiously of the yellowish fluid with chunks.

"I think that, along with the bones and whatever meat is left, it will make a fine stew for later."

"Something else you learned in the Boy Scouts?" she asked.

"You might say." He winked. "Growing up, the nights I spent in the woods were some of my most formative."

He then proceeded to regale her with a story about how he and some of the other kids went to a camp thought to be haunted and just about pissed themselves when some of the older kids decided to pretend they were psycho murderers out to get them. A good, screaming time was had by all. Except for Kelvin. Well into his thirties, he still slept with a nightlight.

"That is way more exciting than anything I ever did," she admitted. "The only time I ever did anything outdoorsy like that was in my backyard with my brother. We found a pup tent someone was tossing out."

"You're close to your brother?" he asked as he tested the meat, not worried so much about the rawness for him but more so for her.

"Yes. Was. Kind of." She sighed. "He's the reason I'm in Russia. He came here months ago to work, and while not the most reliable guy when it comes to communicating, he usually manages to get some kind of word out to me."

"He's missing?" he asked to clarify.

"Yeah."

"How long?"

"Seven months since I last heard from him. At least five that I know for sure he's been gone. The junk mail really started piling up about a month before that, though."

"Wait a second, you came to Russia to find your brother? Alone?" Because she obviously wasn't native to the place.

Her expression tightened. "You think I'm stupid."

"I think you must love him very much." And yes, she was a little dumb, but only for the best reasons.

Her shoulders sagged. "I just wish I knew if he was okay."

"Have you made any progress in your search?"

"What search? I don't know anyone. I thought maybe someone at his building or job would have answers, but no one would talk to me." Her lips curved even lower. "It's like he never existed."

The sheer weariness of the statement tore at him. He had to ease that weight. "When we get out of here, I'd like to help."

Her gaze rose to meet his. "Why?"

"Because family is everything. I recently had a cousin go missing, so I know how that feels."

"Did you find them?"

"Yes. Miriam came back to us." He left out the part where she was shot and tossed in a river to die. She'd recovered but would always have a scar.

"It's been so long since I've heard from Peter."

"Don't give up hope. Not until you know for sure. I'll help you get answers when we get out of here."

"You are way more confident about that happening than I am." A rueful admission.

"Don't you worry, Peanut. I'll get you back to civilization in one piece." He pulled the pan from the fire and shook it to roll the charred meat in the juices. "Dinner is served."

Not much was said as they chowed down. He didn't eat much, having already partaken outside while in his liger form. It meant there was enough left to throw in a pot with the can of stew and some more snow.

"Soup for breakfast?" she quipped as she stirred the pot.

"Wait until you see what I plan for lunch." He lay on the sleeping bag, feet aimed at the fire, hands crossed under his head.

"You don't think we'll be rescued before then." Stated, not asked.

"We could try walking out, but that will be miserable in that snow. Our best bet is to wait."

"Wait for someone to rescue us?" She snorted. "I wish I shared your optimism."

"Are you always this pessimistic?"

"I'm a realist. And as a person who's been clumsy her entire life, I always have to look for the worst."

"You need someone to catch you."

"I do not. I—" She whirled to rebut his claim, her ankles got confused, and the next thing they both knew, she landed in his arms. Proving his point.

"I think you should have a seat."

"I agree. I'm tired," she muttered, her cheeks hot. He shifted her so she could sit on the pillow beside him. Rather than park her sweet ass in it, she gestured. "You're the one lying down. You should put the pillow under your head."

A soft cushion would be nice, but a man should always strive to be a gentleman. "You found it and were using it first."

"We'll share." She flopped the cushion down beside his head, and then inched herself down in a way that gave her an edge of it without any part of her body touching his and put her back to him.

Invitation to spoon? Or, more likely, her way of shutting him out? He might have been more offended if he hadn't caught whiffs of her arousal or the way heat sometimes stained her cheeks when she peeked at him.

It was a few minutes of silence before he dared to sigh and say, "I can't sleep." He could tell by her breathing she didn't either.

Rather than pretend, she accepted the opening and made conversation. "Were you afraid you'd get lost when you went hunting?"

"I've got good sense of direction."

"Even in a storm?" she asked.

How to explain that he now apparently had a lodestone to orient him. A mate. No one ever told him they acted like a compass. Would it work in reverse? Would she know when he went to the bar?

He side-eyed her. She was human. It probably wasn't the same.

He didn't know, and she wanted an answer to her original query. "Given the shit visibility, I didn't stray too far."

She shifted in place. "Who do you think used to own this place?"

"Probably a guy looking for peace and quiet."

She craned her head, trying to look back at him. "Why a guy? Who says it's not a girl?"

"Just a gut feel. And a lack of books."

"What does books have to do with anything?" Apparently tired of trying and failing at the exorcism head spin, she rolled on the pillow to eye him.

"Guys who go off in the woods by themselves don't read. They clean their guns. Fix their traps. Oil and sharpen stuff." He should know. He'd done it.

"Meaning women are lazy."

"No, just more efficient in the daytime. You multitask better most of the time, so at night, you all have time to read."

Her lips rounded in the most delightful way. "That is ridiculously sexist."

It was, but he did point out, "It's a compliment that you're smarter than guys."

"Calling women book nerds is—" She pursed her lips. "Okay, so it's not an insult, but it is a generalization."

"So what you're saying is you wouldn't bring a book to a cabin?"

"I never said that. I would totally bring a book, or two, maybe a wheelbarrow full. But that's not the point. I'm not every woman."

"You agree and yet won't say you agree. And right there, that is why I will never understand women," he grumbled.

"We're complex," she admitted.

"I'm not." It was a strange thing to admit to his Peanut, and yet it caused her to have the most contemplative expression.

"A day ago, I would have agreed and said you were a simple playboy, flashy exterior, shallow interior."

"But now?" he asked softly.

"You're maybe not as vain and annoying as I thought."

"Careful with that wild praise, my head might explode," he teased. Something tickled his cheek.

He would have thought nothing of it, but her eyes widened in horror and she screamed almost loud enough to shatter his eardrums. Charlotte scrambled from their spot, dancing and yelling.

At first, he thought she was screaming, "Fire," then realized it was spider.

Oh, the tickly thing. He swept the insect from his body.

But that only made her yodeling worse.

Afraid of a spider? Ridiculous. Everyone knew it was those nasty ticks you had to watch for.

Even after he put the eight-legged devil outside, she sat huddled with her knees to her chest, eyeing the room suspiciously.

"It's gone. You can lie down."

"I can't. Did you see the size of it? You know they say we swallow at least one spider a year. I'd choke if it tried to crawl into my mouth."

"It is not surviving that storm to return."

"It probably has friends.

"I'll protect you."

"I'd rather just go home," she wailed.

"You will. Soon. But you can't stay awake the entire time. Come here." He patted the spot on the pillow beside him.

She lay down, tucked close enough it gave a man ideas. He wouldn't act on them, though. There was a time and place for seduction. While a woman was scared wasn't one of them, and while some would say a cottage with a roaring fire was romantic, he doubted either of them would enjoy the hard floor.

Pity the place didn't come with a bear rug. But they did have a blanket folded to the side. He shook it out, made sure it had no eight-legged surprises, and then draped it over her.

Her happy sigh was worth the effort. He lay back behind her, not touching, even if he wanted to.

"Do you have enough blanket?" she asked suddenly.

"I don't need one."

"Meaning no." She squirmed and wiggled and tugged at that blanket until some of it covered him. It left her closer than before by the time it was all said and done. Her back was to his chest, but she kept her bottom just out of each.

Her scent filled his senses. Calmed him even as it excited.

It must have proved soothing to her, too, because she murmured a drowsy, "Shouldn't one of us stay awake to fend off spiders?"

"Don't worry. I'll keep watch."

He woke to her shrill scream.

CHAPTER EIGHT

This time Charlotte didn't wake up smooshed under Lawrence but spooned against him. An admittedly comfy spot, especially the weight of his arm over her. However, nice as it was, she had to pee something fierce. All that melted snow she'd drunk had gone through her.

The wind that howled a disharmonious symphony the night before had died down, and light crept in around the edges of the shutters. They'd made it through the night; however, having to pee brought a glaring problem into view. Either she squatted in a corner or she had to go outside.

Since she would probably die of embarrassment if he caught her pissing on the floor, she chose outside, but that meant first getting away from him without waking him up.

She took her time shimmying free. He grunted a few times, even tightened his arm at once point, but eventually she managed to get out of their warm nest. She immediately shivered. The fire had sputtered into embers. The cold began to seep and win against the warmth.

Lawrence rolled and muttered a very sleepy, "Whatcha doing?"

Not telling him the truth, that was for sure. "Putting a log on the fire."

A plausible excuse. She snared a piece and, rather than toss it like him, placed it inside the hearth.

"Put two," was his advice before he started snoring again.

She quickly slipped on her coat and shoes then grasped the door. The first creak made his snore sputter.

She froze. He settled, and she pulled the door all the way open.

Damn it was bright. All that white plus sunshine made for squinty conditions. She stumbled through the snow, at least a foot of fresh stuff, leaving a clear trail, but she didn't have much of a choice. She walked around the side of the cottage before she finally popped a squat. The handful of snow she used to wipe herself clean just about froze her bits, and she hastily pulled up her pants.

She didn't want to think of what she'd do when number two hit. The sudden tumble of snow off the roof hit her in a cold avalanche and drew a scream, especially since it found that crack between neckline and skin and fell down her back.

As she stumbled back to the cottage, her feet and shoes soaked and cold, she saw Lawrence standing in the doorway. Leaning against it. Disheveled. The good start to a beard on his jaw. And way sexier than she felt with her messy hair and pasty mouth.

"Everything okay? I heard you scream. Did you use the wrong kind of leaf to wipe?"

Might as well die right now. He knew she'd peed. "No leaf. I used snow."

"That must have been cold. I'll grab you something better when I go foraging."

"No need."

"Don't be polite. I know where there's a stash of leaves that we could use. Not exactly Charmin soft, but it will do for the moment."

"Can we stop talking about it? Please?"

"I'd rather not." He grinned. "Your face. Priceless."

Which only served to make her cheeks hotter. "Not funny."

"Everyone has to go." He winked. "I had an aunt who used to read me a story about it."

"Again, really would rather not talk about it."

"What should we chat about then?"

"The storm is gone."

"Leaving behind a good foot of snow. Your point is?"

"We should leave while it's daylight."

"You wouldn't make it a mile before you lost those cute toes." He pointed to her feet.

"I was fine when you kidnapped me the last time," she retorted.

"That was an emergency. This time, we're going to sit back and relax and wait for the cavalry."

"What if they don't come?"

"Then hope for an early spring. I don't know about you, but I am feeling grimy." He proceeded to strip off his shirt then fell straight onto the snow.

"What are you doing?"

"What's it look like I'm doing?" He waved his arms and legs and even rolled his head.

"Are you making a snow angel?" She couldn't help the incredulous note.

"As if I'd do something so childish," he scoffed. "I am merely flattening an area in front of our residence while, at the same time, cleansing my skin by scouring it with ice crystals."

"That is a load of bull," she exclaimed, but she laughed.

"Is it? You should try it."

"It's too cold to strip."

"It's refreshing." He bounced to his feet and turned to show her his back, the skin moist with melted snow. The spot he'd smushed in his churning more of a hulking cloaked demon than angel. "Now for the front."

He wasn't—

He did. Took those pants right off, underpants too, showed her a butt that was just as sun kissed as the rest of him. He toppled face first into the pristine snow and once more got freaky.

She had to glance away rather than wonder if he was having some serious shrinkage issues. She crouched and grabbed a handful of snow, using it to rub against her face, grimy with soot and dust. Her already chilly skin didn't get as dewy wet as his.

"Want to melt some so you can do a proper sponge bath at the sink?"

Did she ever! She whirled to accept and then forgot how to speak. For one, he was closer than expected. Two... Her gaze dropped.

Still very, very naked. And not affected by the snow.

Oh my.

"You weren't kidding about being comfortable in the nude," she muttered, the heat in her face not just from embarrassment.

"You might say my entire family is pretty blasé about it. Nudity isn't a big deal for us."

"More for some than others I'll bet." She kept her gaze averted from his groin.

He grinned. "A lot more for some."

"Aren't you cold?"

"I tend to run hot, so I handle these kinds of temps better than other folks."

"Could you at least put on some underpants?"

"Such a prude. But if it makes you feel better..."

She didn't wait for him to dress but fled into the cottage where she shed her snow-filled boots and aimed her damp, cold toes at the fire.

He entered a while later with an armful of leaves that he dropped into a pile by the wood. "I'll make sure to grab more later if the stash gets low."

She changed the subject. "I'm starving. Think that soup is good?"

It was delicious, thick and hearty, and it lined their bellies. When he went out hunting, she opened a set of shutters and washed the window enough to get some clear light.

She washed some more. Humming and oddly content. She had so many things to worry her right now, yet she found serenity in righting the cottage and making it homier. She even managed to bite her tongue when something scurried across the floor—and died as she slammed it over and over with her broom.

When Lawrence returned, it was with more nuts and a few fat birds. Dinner would be epic.

And with the feathers, few as there were, he made her a cushion for her bum. If this had been an actual date, it would have rated an eleven out of ten.

Except for all the flirting, Lawrence never crossed a line. It made the bite all the more incongruous. He must have really been drugged out of his mind to have done it.

As they ate, she smiled at his antics, laughed at his jokes, and actually had fun. She realized, despite her first impressions, she had a man worthy of her attention right in front of her.

He caught her staring as he did their dishes after dinner.

"What? What did I do now?" he asked in mock fear.

"I do not chastise you that often."

"I know, which is why I sometimes do it on purpose to get you going."

"You like making me mad?"

"I enjoy everything about you, Peanut."

"Oh." There was no reply to that.

"Do you have a boyfriend?"

It came out of nowhere, and she blurted out, "No," before she could think twice.

"Good."

"Why good?"

"Because you don't seem like the type to cheat."

"I'm not. I wouldn't. I mean... You're doing it again," she huffed. "Getting me flustered."

"What are you going to do about it?"

An interesting question. She could bluster and blush, but he would just keep on teasing. She had to find a better way to handle him. A way to shove him off balance.

Perhaps she needed a drastic change in her tactics. Leaving the dishes spread out to dry, he joined her on the blanket.

She leaned close and kissed him. A quick brush of her mouth but it still caused him to draw in a sharp breath.

"What was that for?" Lawrence asked.

"Because I was curious."

"About?"

Admit her fascination with him? How he made her tingle head to toe? More importantly, did he make anyone else tingle? "Do you have a girlfriend or wife?"

"Not exactly."

"Meaning what?" Had she just kissed a married man?

"It's complicated." A crooked grin that did nothing to help her inner deflation.

"So you are taken."

He shook his head and reached for her hands, their

warmth causing a deep awareness. He drew her close. "Trust me when I say I am available for anything you might desire."

Pretty words. Cheating words. She pulled her hands free. "I will not be the other woman."

"You wouldn't be. I mean I'm not with anyone but you."

"I don't believe you."

"I'm not the type to step out on a woman."

"Says you. How many women have you dated?"

His lips flattened. "I don't see how that's relevant." The implicating being too many for him to comfortably mention.

"What's the longest you've ever been with someone?"

"How long for you?" he riposted.

"I once managed four and a half years."

"Why did you break up?"

"His penis fell into someone else. And you still haven't answered me. What's the longest you've been with someone?"

She didn't specify so he played dumb. "I've been friends with Dean for over a decade. And I'm still talking to most of my family."

Her expression chastised.

He slumped. "I once managed six months." Only because she lived in a different country. It only took a few in-person visits before they broke up.

"Six months." She blinked at him. "What is wrong with you?"

He gaped. "What makes you think I'm the problem?"

"You're too pretty. No girl is going to break up with you that quick unless you're a real jerk. Or..." She halted.

He prodded. "Or what?"

"You're really, really bad at *you know*." She tried to sound meaningful.

He choked. "No. You did not just accuse me of being a terrible lover. I'll have you know I've never left a woman dissatisfied."

"How would you know? You practically admitted you rarely go back for seconds. How do you even know they're interested?"

This time he blinked. "Because they ask me for more."

"Again, I'm going to remind you of the whole pretty thing. Could be some of them hoped you weren't as bad as they recalled."

His expression was finally off balance in a way that had her unable to control the snickering.

"Wait a second. Are you fucking with me?"

"Nope. I hear you might be bad at it."

"Why you minx." He sounded amused rather than indignant. He lunged for her, and she didn't quite make it out of reach. His fingers dug into her ribs and found her ticklish spots.

She laughed hard and uncontrollably. She writhed but couldn't quite escape and didn't really want to either. Odd given he'd just admitted he was a one-and-done kind of guy.

Perhaps that was what appealed. Sex with no strings. Just a physical release. It had been so long since she'd had that kind of contact with anyone.

Something in their tickling wrestling match changed, became charged. They both stilled. She sat atop him, straddling his midsection, her hands on his chest. His fingers, now still, gripped her by the waist.

She leaned down and kissed him. Not a short peck. Not a simple fluttery brush of lips.

She kissed him open mouth, hot breath, and exploding passion that saw her rolled to her back. He half lay across her, taking a shy exploration into a sizzling territory that ignited all her nerve endings.

The fire in the hearth crackled, but it didn't kick out half the heat her desire did. She clung to his broad shoulders and enjoyed each nibbling bite. Half swooned when their tongues twined.

When his lips began tracing a path down, she undulated and gasped. She didn't say a word but rather helped him strip off her blouse. He pushed aside the cups on her bra that he might rub his raspy jaw on the tender skin. He nuzzled. Licked. Sucked on the very tip, drawing pleasurable jolts through her that soon had her panting.

He inserted his thigh between her legs as he toyed with her breasts, the hard line of it giving her something to squirm against. To catch her breath and feel the languor spread.

When his hand slipped past the waistband of her pants, her legs parted further to give his questing fingers access. He cupped her and rumbled around the nipple in his mouth, "Wet."

Very wet.

He dipped a finger inside her. Two. Long fingers that knew where to reach and stroke. He soon had her writhing and bucking, her hips lifting to meet his hand, his mouth sucking hard at her nipples and biting them on occasion for that extra jolt.

When she came, her back arched and her pelvic muscles clenched. He'd lost his grip on her breast and went for her mouth, his kiss hot and possessive.

Her body throbbed in sated orgasmic bliss. He kept stroking her, drawing out the climax, stoking it and building it up.

When he positioned himself over her, she was ready. More than ready.

Her hands went to her pants to lower them, only he vaulted off her, suddenly bristling with tension.

"What's wrong?" she asked.

"Stay here." He didn't bother to add any layers or even his shoes. He stalked out of the hut, wearing only his pants and nothing else as he shut the door behind him.

The abrupt switch from lover to guy on alert had her scrambling to put on her blouse then her coat and shoes for good measure. She stuffed the extra nuts into her pockets just in case they had to run.

Minutes ticked by. He didn't return.

She didn't hear a damned sound but for the crackle of the fire.

Exiting the cabin, she realized twilight encroached. No sign of Lawrence.

He wouldn't have just left her. Not without his clothes.

Perhaps he'd gone to check a trap. Surely he wouldn't have bothered in the midst of... She blushed to think of it, and her lower parts twitched. Since she didn't want him to think she was looking for him, she grabbed some leaves and headed for the spot around the side. She'd discovered earlier that the woodpile made for a decent cover so that she was barely exposed.

The leaves didn't feel as good as the snow probably would have on her hot flesh. The darkness cloaked the ground quickly as the sun dipped below the tree line.

Still no Lawrence.

She was about to go back inside when it appeared at the edge of the woods—a giant cat. Had to be a cougar. Or a mountain lion. The species didn't matter. She would wager it was hungry.

As it stalked toward her, it was joined by two more. They circled her, gazes intent, their low rumbles a warning of what was to come.

She'd survived kidnapping and a blizzard, just had the best orgasm of her life, and was now about to get eaten by the wildlife. Wait, had they already killed Lawrence?

The thought saddened her even if she barely knew him. But she couldn't let it affect her. Not when her life was also on the line. She wasn't going to die easily or quietly. She bolted for the door of the cabin, and the cats pounced in the snow, one of them pulling ahead to cut her off.

Oh shit.

She backed against the cabin wall, trying to keep all three cats in view. One of them stalked forward. Trembling like a leaf in a storm, Charlotte froze. The cat shoved its face right in her crotch.

That drew a loud shriek, which led to another cat suddenly bounding into the clearing. It was a massive striped lion that roared, and then the lion was Lawrence bellowing, "What the fuck are you doing, you crazy old cats? Stop scaring my Peanut."

"Spoilsport."

Charlotte blinked, and yet the giant cat with its golden fur had disappeared and, in its place, stood a giant-sized woman who was very naked.

The other two felines were suddenly humans in the buff, too, and Charlotte realized she must be dreaming. Or having a nightmare. Something. Because people did not go from cat to contorting impossibly into human beings.

"Peanut." Lawrence's soft tone drew her attention. "Look at me. You're okay." He snared his pants from a bush, and began pulling them on.

"This isn't real," she muttered. "People aren't cats." The expired soup must be at fault.

"Not all people. Only shapeshifters."

She stared at him and shook her head. "Shapeshifters don't exist."

"I'd say you just saw proof they do."

"No. That wasn't real. Cats don't turn into people. You are not a lion. This is a dream. Nightmare. Maybe there is no cottage at all, and we never escaped the forest." She babbled as she sidled along the edge of the cottage, looking to put some distance between her and the naked people. She was feeling overdressed and very confused. "Maybe I'm in a hypothermic coma and imagining this is happening."

"You're not dreaming, Peanut. I know this seems a little strange." He finished buttoning his bottoms, but remained barefoot and chested in the snow.

"A little?" A hysterical giggled bubbled from her. "You were a giant freaking lion!"

"I'm a liger actually."

"A what?"

"I'm what you call a hybrid. Part lion, part tiger."

"Of course you are." She finally found out the reason why he couldn't hold on to a woman. He liked to pretend he was an animal. "Let me guess, these women belong to the same crazy commune."

"Actually, we're his aunts. And who are you?" the woman with the darkest hair, streaked in gray, demanded haughtily.

Lawrence did the introductions. "Aunties, this is Charlotte. Charlotte, Aunt Lena, Aunt Lenore, and Aunt Lacey." He pointed them out, one by one.

"You're related to him," she stated.

"His father was our brother," said the biggest of the aunts.

"Much older brother," clarified the blondest of the three. "I'm Lacey by the way. Chubby is Lenore, and the one with the trucker mouth is Lena."

"Rather speak how it is than be all fake," scowled Lena, tossing her messy silver hair.

Lenore of the dark hair and light streaks, and the one to sniff her crotch, frowned. "Lawrence, is that—"

Before his aunt could finish, he threw himself at her, hugging her, which Charlotte would admit was weird.

Half-naked nephews did not hug naked aunts. Or turn into lions. Had he put some mushrooms in their soup?

"You have one seriously messed-up family," was the last thing she said before she shoved past the naked Amazon lady and into the cottage to check for drugs.

CHAPTER NINE

"You better start talking, and fast," threatened Aunt Lenore.

"Nice to see you, too," he drawled.

"Don't you sass me." Lena shook a finger at him, and while a human might have been uncomfortable being confronted by three naked family members, shifters didn't have the same taboos about nudity. For them, skin was like fur, and clothes were simply a costume they had to wear to pretend they were human.

"I'm sorry. I should have said thank you for coming to my rescue. You arrived a tad quicker than expected, though." He thought he'd have until later tonight or the following morning at least.

"Are you calling us old and slow?" Lenore took offense at a perceived slight.

Rather than clarify, he teased. "Well, you have started wearing slippers."

"They aren't just any slippers but unicorn flamingoes," she stated, lifting her chin. "I like them 'cause they're cute. That doesn't make me old."

"Yeah it does," coughed Lena, earning a glare.

Lacey stepped in before it went any further. "Now isn't the time, sisters."

"Yeah, we should get back to our dumb-ass nephew and the fact he is not in danger but shacking up."

"Wish we'd known that before we commandeered those snowmobiles," grumbled Lenore.

The mention pricked Lawrence's attention. "Are they far? I thought I heard engines." Having the machines would make their trek back out a lot quicker.

"As if you heard us coming," scoffed Lenore. "We parked about a mile away."

"A mile? Not too far, then."

"We thought you might be in trouble and snuck in," Lacey explained.

"I was in trouble but managed to get out. On my own," he emphasized.

"Well la di da for you. Guess we'll just turn around and leave then."

The aunts as one lifted their chins and acted as if they'd depart. And they would, too, if he didn't say the magic words. "While I did escape my initial capture, I could use your help getting out of these woods."

"What's that?" Lena asked. "I don't think I heard you."

"I said please help."

"Not until you tell us what happened. Who is that girl?" Lenore demanded.

"I'd like to know, too. There's something about her..." Lacey trailed off as she glanced at the cottage.

"Something strange yet familiar," Lena added.

"You nitwits. Are ya fucking blind?" Lenore swore. Apparently, she'd seen what the others hadn't. "She had marks on her neck." She squinted at him. "You mated her!"

"He what?" screeched Lacey. Probably more pissed he'd done it without letting her plan a wedding first. Having only a nephew didn't stop his aunt from starting a wedding scrapbook—over which he had little control.

Lenore nodded. "He did. He bit that girl—"

"Woman," he corrected, earning another glare.

"Human," was Lena's correction, and he winced.

"Well, that would explain why she smells funny," was Lacey's contribution.

He thought she had the most enticing scent.

"He can't be mated," argued Lena. "The boy is like us, free spirited."

"Was," Lenore corrected. "I know what I saw."

"Lies!" Lena hissed.

"I don't think so. Look at his face." His aunt Lacey didn't look any happier, but she did soften her tone as she said, "Tell us, Roarie." She used her pet name for him. Because apparently as a baby he had the cutest mewling roar. "Tell us what happened."

Admit what he'd done? His aunts would probably go ballistic. Lie and they'd probably do something to his Peanut. "First promise no one gets hurts. Not me and especially not her."

For a moment, he thought they might refuse. Lena

opened her mouth, but Lacey put her hand on her arm and gave a slight shake of her head.

"We promise, no harm to the woman." Lean scowled.

"Her name is Charlotte." Best they start seeing her as a person right now. An important person. He already knew it wouldn't go over well. It never did.

"Charlotte as in a wily spider who dragged you into her web?" Lena eyed the cabin suspiciously. "Did she force you to mark her?"

"Hardly," was his dry reply. "She has no idea what the bite means."

It was Aunt Lenore who cuffed him. "You bloody idiot! You broke the rule!" The one that said no biting unless the other person was aware of what it meant.

"There were extenuating circumstances," he grumbled. "It happened by accident while I was under the influence of drugs."

"You got high and bit the girl?" Lenore screeched. "I thought we taught you better."

He ducked the cuff to the head and quickly replied, "I didn't take the drugs on purpose. The people who abducted us injected me with something."

That paused the waving paw of his aunt Lenore. She frowned. "Someone kidnapped you?"

"How is it we're just hearing about it?" Lena barked.

And that was when he got his best dig. "Perhaps if you'd located me faster... Noticed when your precious nephew, like a son, went missing..."

"How were we supposed to know you weren't tomcatting?" complained Lena.

"You keep saying you want your space," added Lacey.

"It's obviously because I am just not loved." He sighed theatrically.

Lenore snorted. "You are such a little shit."

He winked. "Learned from the best."

"You did, which is how I know you're stalling rather than explaining." Lenore snapped her fingers. "Let's hear the rest of it."

"Rest of what? I wasn't myself when I marked her."

"And were you still drugged when you were f—"

"Lena!" Lacey shrieked. "Don't you dare say it."

"Fine, I won't because we can all smell it. And I think someone needs to be explaining how, if the bite was an accident, he ended up in her pants."

Admitting he couldn't help himself would result in his aunts making more tomcat remarks. Instead, he chose to explain how he got to the cabin. "So I was kidnapped during the reception..." He embellished the story and had the men armed with cattle prods as well as guns. He went on to tell about the mysterious boss lady, her conviction he knew where a certain object could be found, and the fact they possessed the kind of drugs meant to make him talk. A drug that appeared to have unintended consequences for shifters. Was his reaction an anomaly or something they should be aware of?

Aunt Lacy appeared thoughtful. "I've heard of a few plants that can have that kind of blackout effect on us, but nothing as long-lived as you experienced."

"Some kind of ultra-version then," Lenore remarked.

"We'll have to track down what they used and let our scientists play with it."

Because a danger to one was a danger to all.

"Anyhow, I woke up here, just before the storm hit," he continued.

"And didn't go far once it passed on." Lena cocked her head.

"I thought about it, but I worried about Charlotte's ability to withstand the cold and snow. I figured it best to wait for your arrival."

"That explains why you had the dirtiest fire in existence burning. Could see and smell it for miles," Lena complained.

"As if you needed help. When did the satellite pick up my location?" Because his aunts chipped and tracked him after that weeklong binge in his early twenties that had them freaking.

"We picked up your signal the afternoon after the party mostly on account we didn't get worried until around lunchtime when you didn't wander back to the hotel. We all know how much you hate sleeping over." Aunt Lenore knew him well.

Sleeping over led to talk and expectations he preferred to avoid. He really was a jerk. But in his defense, he'd tried to date longer than a couple of times with the last few women he'd met. Three dates to six dates. That was the maximum he managed before he had to move on.

"If you saw it that afternoon, we were still at the farm. We must have just missed each other."

"Not exactly," Lacey said sourly. "Someone was in a mood and didn't want to go on a road trip."

"It was a ride to the middle of nowhere. Of course I didn't want to go," huffed Lenore.

"Given the delay," Lacey continued, "we didn't leave until around noon the next day, when we realized your signal had moved to some unpopulated woods."

His brows rose. "And that was when you finally got worried? Feeling so loved."

"Stop it. You're fine. And aren't you the one who keeps saying you're a big boy?" Lena reminded. "Still, knowing you're an idiot, we decided to check in on you and arrived at the farm just as the storm hit. Not that it would have mattered much. There was nothing to find in the ruins."

"What ruins?"

"Place was set on fire, probably right after you left, given the ashes were fresh. Between how hard it burned and the snow, we didn't find shit." Lenore grimaced. She took her tracking seriously.

"And as my loving aunts, you just knew I was alive and still in trouble rather than dead."

"I did," Lena insisted. "But that one was sobbing like a baby." She pointed at Lacey.

"Because some of us have hearts."

"Pussy."

"C—"

Lenore cleared her throat. "I reminded them that your tracker put you farther than the farmhouse."

"But that didn't mean he was alive," Lacey insisted.

"Dead people don't make smoke," he reminded.

"Didn't mean it was you. For all we knew, someone was having a giant barbecue. We had no idea who lit that fire until we got close." Lacey clasped her hands, her worry obvious.

Lena shook her head. "Still can't believe you'd mark your position in such an obvious way. You had to know we'd find you without it."

"Charlotte was cold," he explained.

Three sets of eyes stared him down, but it was Lenore who softly said, "And? If you mated her by accident, then letting her succumb to the elements would have been an easy choice."

Easy yes, but not an option, and rather than explain that, he changed the subject. "Where did you manage to rent sleds?"

"We didn't exactly rent them," Lena admitted.

"Meaning you stole them." Lawrence sighed. "What have I told you?"

The scowl on Lena's face went well with her sighed, "We should ask first."

"Exactly, because people tend to be happier if you give them money rather than just taking their stuff."

"Sharing is caring," Lena huffed. "And we only need them for a few hours. They should be happy they're doing us a favor."

"Of course, they should." He wanted to bang his head on a wall. His aunts truly lived in their own world.

"Don't let him chastise us," Lenore barked. "He's the one who's still in trouble. He mated that girl."

"Charlotte."

"Whatever. You marked a human."

"I wasn't in my right mind."

"And then made it worse by...by..."

Lacey couldn't say it, so Lena crudely did. "Making her yowl. Meaning any chance of breaking the bond is definitely toast."

"I didn't mean to," he said, only to realize he didn't really mind. Something about his Peanut had him acting strangely. Feeling different.

"Too late for regrets now," snorted Lena. "For better or worse, you're tied together. Until death do you part."

"Need help with that part?" Lenore asked, cracking her knuckles.

"No. What I need is for you to fetch those snowmobiles while I try to figure out how to explain all this to Charlotte." She'd not looked impressed when she'd stalked into the hut.

"Explain?" Lena doubled over laughing. "How you gonna explain that not only are you a big fucking liger but she's your wife?"

The door flung open. "His what?"

He shriveled harder than the time he jumped into that glacier-fed lake. "I can explain."

CHAPTER TEN

"I highly doubt any of you can explain this." Because Charlotte certainly couldn't comprehend how lions turned into naked ladies. And before anyone was mistaken, she didn't mean the bare-naked singing kind but the steely-eyed, would rip her to shreds with their fingernails kind.

And Lawrence was not only related but one of them. What kind of freak had she hooked up with?

She wished she'd stayed to listen rather than storming off inside the cabin, only to realize her angry pacing and the sound of the crackling fire meant she couldn't understand what was being said. Voices rose and fell while she was still coming to grips with what she'd seen.

Except there was no understanding it. People weren't animals. And vice versa. They must have been wearing costumes that they flung off to confront her.

And what of Lawrence? He'd left wearing pants and returned naked because he'd changed out of his liger costume. Except she didn't remember seeing any costumes on the ground.

"I know things seem a little strange right now, Peanut."

"A little? I think we're well past a little, Lawrence." She stressed his formal name.

"If you'd like his full name, it's Lawrence Gerome Luke Walker," offered the one called Lena, her hair a short, ruffled cut that appeared a mix of gold and gray. Her features were weathered, yet attractive.

All the women had a beauty to them, and she would know since she kept her gaze on their faces. "Who are you?" she asked.

"I'm Lena. His favorite aunt," Ruffle Cut offered.

The one with darker tresses and a silver streak snorted. "Please, we all know that's me. I'm his aunt Lenore. He's probably mentioned me."

"Only if he wanted to chase her away and he obviously didn't. Ignore them, dearest. I'm his favorite aunt, Lacey. My sisters just can't stand to see our boy getting serious with anyone. I'm sure your mother is the same with you."

"I don't have a mother."

"Well, that will make things easier," Lacey said, earning a rebuke from Lawrence.

"Aunt Lacey!"

"What?" She blinked innocently.

Charlotte had no idea what Lawrence meant when he hissed, "Don't you dare start."

"Who, me?"

The innocent batting of the lashes had him groaning. "You have that devious look in your eye."

"Don't know what you mean." Lacey eyed Charlotte up and down before asking, "Do you have a favorite color?"

"What?"

"Don't tell her!" Lawrence barked, a look of panic in his gaze.

"Really, Roarie, how else will I adjust my binder if I don't ask?"

"What binder?" she asked.

"The wedding one of course. Because you will be repeating your vows in front of friends and family."

"Maybe he doesn't want to perform in front of an audience," Lena declared.

"I'm not marrying your nephew," was Charlotte's contribution.

"After what he did to you, that's kind of a foregone conclusion, dearie."

How did they know? Did it matter? Her cheeks heated. "I don't know what hillbilly religious cult you're from, but the fact we fooled around doesn't mean we're married. As a matter of fact, once I get out of these woods, I don't plan on seeing him ever again."

For some reason this brought first gaping mouths, then intense laughter.

"Oh, this is going to be fun," snickered Lenore.

"We should go and let them have some privacy to talk," Lacey stated, tugging at the other women.

"I want to stay and listen." Lena dug in her heels.

"Give the boy some space." Lacey dragged, and the

aunts moved off. They started out as leggy women and morphed into lions.

Charlotte blinked.

Nope, still giant cats, which took precedence over her supposed marriage to Lawrence. "What is going on? Am I dreaming?"

"No."

"But how... Is it magic? Are your aunts witches or something?"

"No. Even if they do at times cackle. Like I tried to tell you before, they're shapeshifters."

"Meaning they can turn into anything they like."

"Just lions," he corrected. "Shifters tend to only have one beast inside. Unless they're hybrids, then sometimes you can tilt the balance depending on will and strength."

"Hold on, you said shifters. Implying there are more of you?"

"There are quite a few species, actually."

"Like wolves."

"And bears. A few decades ago it included eagles, but given they're almost extinct due to the avian flu, those are the main groups."

She rubbed her forehead. "Your aunts are shifters and so are you."

He nodded and, before she could ask, showed her. One minute big man, the next a massive cat. He wasn't like anything she'd ever seen. His body and fluffy mane were mostly lion-like, but there was some striping in his fur, like that of a tiger.

She rocked on her heels and held in an urge to bolt. "I can't believe it. You're a bloody werelion." And if they were anything like the werewolves of legend... Her eyes widened as her hand slapped her neck. "Fucking asshole. You bit me. Does this mean I'm going to turn into an animal, too?"

He changed back before he could reply. "We're not contagious."

"Says you. Have you had your shots?"

"No need. Shifters in general tend to be quite healthy."

"Isn't that lovely for you." Not to mention she only had his word she wouldn't become a monster on the full moon.

"Listen, I know this is a lot to take in."

"Gee, do you think?" Her sarcasm rolled heavily off the tongue. "So how are werelions made anyhow? Do you even have parents? Or are those aunts like people who took you in once you turned out to be a furball?" Because she still had a hard time grasping that any of this was real. If people were having litters, wouldn't the world know about it?

"They're my family. They raised me after my parents died. Do you think I'd let them stalk and treat me like they do otherwise?"

Her shoulders rolled. "Apparently I don't know much anymore."

"Ah, Peanut." His soft name for her purred. "Don't take it so hard. We're good at keeping our secrets."

"So why tell me?" And not just tell her but shove it in her face. They'd made it impossible for her to explain away.

"I meant to break it more gently, but my aunts, as

you've noticed, tend to have their own ideas on how to do things."

"I don't know what they're hoping to accomplish. I don't care what you are. Once I get out of these woods, we won't see each other again." It was the reason she'd been wanton in the cabin, because she could be without worrying about facing him later.

"About that...remember the bite?"

"The one you keep saying won't get infected?" She rubbed it, the skin having already lost the scab and smoothed over. That seemed fast. Perhaps it was more superficial than she'd imagined.

"The bite will fade as it heals, but what it symbolizes won't go away. It marks you as my mate."

"Your what?"

"Mate. Wife. Partner for life."

She blinked before slowly saying, "I don't think so."

"I'm afraid it's already done. Ouch. Fuck. Why are you hitting me?"

"You lying jerk. All this time. Everything out of your mouth. A lie," she yelled as she kept hitting him.

He grabbed her wrists and growled, "Enough."

"No. Not until you tell me this is a big fucking joke."

"Sorry to disappoint," he said flatly. "And no joke. Our futures are tied, Peanut."

"I don't care what biting means to you and your *people*. I did not consent to be your anything."

"I didn't do it on purpose."

"And that makes it better?" She rolled her eyes. "How do we undo it?"

He shrugged.

"That's not an answer."

"You won't like the answer."

"How about I just refuse to be your wife?"

"I don't think you can," he said, with less certainty.

"Don't think?" She snorted. "Obviously you didn't if you thought you could use your good looks and sexual prowess to turn me into some kind of concubine."

"A concubine is a mistress. You're my mate."

The fact that his bold statement made her heart pitter patter meant she retorted a hot, "No, I'm not."

"Listen, I don't know if there's a way to break the bond, but if you want, we can ask for help in finding out."

"From who? More shifters?" She might have sneered.

"I wouldn't say it like that, or their solution to the dilemma will be a shallow grave in a swamp."

That rounded her mouth. "You'd kill me?"

"Not me." His lips thinned, and he didn't elaborate.

Which didn't help the chill that suddenly went through her.

"You're cold." Instantly solicitous, he wrapped his arms around her, and she would have protested the naked man holding her, except it turned out he was actually still quite warm. Her body didn't care he was a big fat liar; she wanted to bask in it.

"Are you going to let someone kill me?" she asked, craning her head.

"No. I'll find a way to fix things. Promise." His head angled, and he stared into the distance. "I hear the aunts coming back."

It was longer before she heard the distant rumble of engines, and then the bouncing beam of headlights announced their arrival. Freedom within reach. So why did she cast a glance at the cabin and actually feel a pang?

"Let's bundle you up, Peanut. It's going to be a chilly ride."

He insisted she wrap herself in the sleeping bag and the blanket, to which she protested, "You need some clothes too." The aunts had arrived wearing tracksuits, boots, jackets, and ridiculous woolen hats with pompons.

"I'll be fine. I can handle the cold better than you."

"Are you implying once more that we're old?" complained Lena over the rumble of her machine. Lacey rode behind her.

"Never. But it is chilly outside if you're wearing only skin." He led Charlotte to Lenore, who sat alone on her snowmobile. "Hold on tight."

"What about you?"

"I could use some exercise." He winked, and then he went from man to lion. He took off running, and she could only stare.

"That's not normal," she muttered.

"Oh, honey, you ain't seen nothing yet. Now hold on tight. The brakes on this thing don't work so good."

Understatement.

They whipped through the forest, narrowly avoiding trees. The danger was extreme enough that she buried her face in Lenore's back. She didn't want to see death coming.

She also didn't need glimpsed reminders of Lawrence.

A shifter.

Wasn't that something from fantasy books and shows? She wanted to deny it, but that would be ignoring the reality right in front of her. More importantly, she needed to understand what this meant to her.

Was she truly mated to a lion? Been chosen by the most handsome and virile man she'd ever met? A hunk who'd made her come...

She shivered, not in cold, and in the distance, something roared.

CHAPTER ELEVEN

Something shivered inside Lawrence, tingled him in a way he'd only recently begun to experience—because of Charlotte.

He'd gone toe to toe with his aunts over her. Would fight tooth and claw if anyone dared say anything. And then, in the direct opposite, he was intensely worried. Mating lasted for life, and yet he'd never managed more than a few weeks in a relationship. How would he manage that long?

A good sign was the fact he'd not yet had his fill of her. Would he feel the same way after he did indulge? Or was it possible he'd finally stop wandering?

He wished he could see the future. Trust in the mating bond. But his aunts raised him to be suspicious. To thrive as a single. Except they weren't truly ever alone. They always had each other. Lawrence used to have Dean at least. And he knew his aunts would never truly leave him. But what he wanted from his Peanut wasn't something he'd ever craved from anyone before.

It excited. It frightened. It confused.

Why did this have to be so complicated?

He strained, all four of his legs pumping as he followed the snowmobile tracks. It felt good to have the fresh air ruffling his fur after the musty cloy of the cabin. His paws slammed the fresh snow, spraying it into the air in a fine film.

To his surprise, the trail emerged at the farm they'd escaped. The scent of smoke lingered in the air, the house a charred ruin. Someone covering their tracks? Or had he accidentally caused the blaze in his escape? He couldn't recall, and it was kind of annoying because it incinerated any clues he might have gleaned about who'd taken them.

He didn't even know the boss lady's name. Or if she'd died that night.

It also made him wonder if that woman was after him or someone else. Racking his brain and replaying some of the conversations made him realize he'd assumed they were after him, but if he eyed it from a different perspective... It might have been Peter, Peanut's brother, they were after all along.

If he were involved with the kind of people who thought nothing of kidnapping and truth serums, then that didn't bode well for Charlotte's brother's health or survival.

He shifted and headed for the trunk of the car, knowing they'd have brought him a clothing kit. Charlotte wasn't saying much, just clutching the blanket and staring at the ruins. She'd shoved her glasses into a pocket for the ride but perched them back on her nose the moment they stopped.

"I take it I didn't do this on my way out?" he remarked, coming up beside her.

She shrugged. "Not that I recall, but kind of hard to see anything when you're upside down without glasses on and bouncing like a sack of potatoes being taken for a brisk jog."

"You are much sexier than a sack of vegetables."

"Do you have a habit of tossing women on your back and taking off with them?"

"You'd be the first."

"And don't worry, you'll probably be his last," remarked his aunt Lena. "If you kids are done doing nothing constructive, get your asses in the car. It's at least an hour to the nearest place with booze and food."

The car was tight and warm with the five of them crammed inside. Some of the heat radiated from his annoyance because Charlotte appeared determined not to have anything to do with him. She chose to sit in the middle of the backseat, but when he would have joined her, she looked past him and said, "I'd prefer your aunt was back here with me."

"Ooh. Now that's a surprise," Aunt Lenore muttered. "Usually the ladies are falling all over themselves to get close to you."

"Not helping," growled Lawrence as he slunk into the front passenger seat.

"Gotta say, I'm starting to like the girl." High compliment from Lena. "She knows to not listen to your bullshit."

To his surprise, Charlotte came to his rescue. "I am starting to see why he has commitment issues. I've heard of apron strings, but you have him raveled in a massive three-twine ball of snarly mess."

The polite rebuke had his aunts gaping at the human who dared accuse them of hovering.

He almost snickered. Especially since she wasn't joking.

Lenore took offense first. "It's not as if we want to be the ones taking care of him."

"But someone has to," Lacey hastily added.

"My sisters are right for once." Lena's addition. "Keep in mind, Roarie is a man, and we all know they need a keeper. It's why I never settled down."

"They expect you to share a closet," was Lacey's horrified admission.

Whereas Lenore said, "I don't mind them, but I tend to intimidate them after awhile."

"Arm wrestling them in public, winning, and telling them to do the yellow-belly walk of shame would send anyone fleeing," Lena said with a snort.

"I'm surprised, given your obviously savvy personalities, that he's so inept at his age," Charlotte said.

The insult, so neatly done, meant his aunts were actually silent for a second before tumbling over each other, suddenly playing up his strong points.

"Oh, he might be dumb sometimes, but the boy is actually brilliant. Mostly B's in college. He would have gotten A's if he applied himself," Lacey chided.

"And handsome. While his father passed at a young age, we can assure you that his granddad seasoned quite nicely. Why, he's still considered the randiest cat down in Florida where he spends all his time now," Lena said.

Lawrence slouched in the seat. The old man was both a tribute and scary precaution of what the future could hold. Grandpa didn't remarry when his wife died. He became a player. Had been for over twenty years now. Did he ever get tired of it?

He glanced at Charlotte, who caught his gaze. Her tone held a hint of a smirk as she said, "Handsome is as handsome does."

"The boy does plenty. He can hunt. Plus, he can play sports. Hand him any ball, glove, or stick, and our nephew will become a pro." Lenore praised him this time.

Torture. The worst kind, as his aunts suddenly appeared determined to make Charlotte like him. But his Peanut proved stubborn.

"Is he good? Or does he just have an advantage most people don't have?" she asked.

"Not his fault he was born perfect." Aunt Lacey sniffed.

"Perfect?" Charlotte laughed. "I'd hardly use that word."

"Then what would you call my nephew?" Lena's tone was quiet. Too quiet.

He kept an eye on her. Just in case.

"I'd say he's a man who feels a need to play a role rather than be himself," Charlotte said.

"No, he's not pretending at being a tom cat. He is a—"

A flick in the back of Lenore's head stopped that in its tracks. But it was still too late.

"You mean a man whore?" Charlotte nodded. "Yup. I can see that. He is much too pretty. I'll bet the girls don't even make him work at it."

"They don't. It's why he gets bored." Lenore agreed.

"Is it because women don't interest him?" Once more Charlotte twisted his aunt's words.

Lacey laughed. "Oh, she is quick."

"Too quick," grumbled Lena.

"Speaking of quick, where are we going at ridiculous speed?" Charlotte asked.

A good question. "Auntie?"

"Told you. We're hungry," Lena grumbled.

"Meaning?"

"Ain't many places out here to find food and drink, maybe a bed for the night, so we don't have much of a choice." Lena appeared to be avoiding a proper reply.

"Why do I get the feeling I won't like this?"

Lenore sighed. "Because you won't. We're going to see the Medvedev."

He pursed his lips. "You've got to be kidding. You do realize they're nuts, right?" The last time he'd run into a bear from the Medvedev sleuth he almost got arrested.

"It will be fine. Stop being such a kitten about it," scoffed Aunt Lena.

"Kitten?" Charlotte bit her lip but didn't manage to completely stem her mirth.

"I know, hard to see him as a youngling now that he's so huge. He's not half as cute as when he was little." Lenore didn't help things.

"Hey!" he protested.

"What? It's the truth. He had the chubbiest cheeks as a baby," Lacey enthused. Then proceeded to show Charlotte because, of course, her phone had pictures, a veritable timeline of his life.

And his Peanut actually looked at them then remarked, "His poor mother. Look at that fat head."

"He was a tubby tabby, all right. From a young age, we had to put him on a protein and exercise regime," Lena said proudly.

The history of his life continued unfolding with every image shared. Charlotte's gaze even strayed to him a few times, not that he was watching—directly at any rate. He was slouched in a way that allowed him to watch her in the rearview mirror.

He didn't take his attention off her until they pulled through some old wrought iron gates set into dark stone arches. The drive was pebbled and lined with trees and led to a roundabout with a massive stone fountain bubbling coldly. A few Jeeps missing doors and roofs and covered in mud and slush were parked randomly.

The house was massive and made of both natural and cut stone. It had the feel of an ancient fortress but sported modern amenities like lights instead of torches. It could have used better air filtration because the moment they walked in his hackles rose.

He hoped against hope that he wouldn't be here.

He must have growled because Charlotte muttered, "What's wrong?"

"Bears."

"What?"

No time to explain as someone bellowed, "Why if it isn't Lawrence the Little Liger, my best friend in the whole wide world. Give me a hug." A massive man ambled for him, and there was no avoiding the hug that attempted to crack his ribs.

"Hello, Andrei," he managed to gasp. No way would he complain. Only pussies couldn't handle a bear hug.

"What a nice surprise. I knew you would forgive me eventually."

"I haven't. My aunts insisted I come." He scowled at the reminder of the last time they'd been together, when he ended up in a prison being stripped and cavity searched. His ass cheeks still clenched at the smell of latex.

Andrei beamed wider. "You brought your aunts? Always did love the older ladies. Are they still single?"

"You want them, have them," he muttered.

"Maybe later, as I smell something delectable. Did you bring me a human snack?" Andrei rubbed his hands. He liked to joke that his family ate the human peasants in the area when the winters were lean. At least, Lawrence hoped they were jesting.

"She is not for you. Her name is Charlotte." And then because he didn't like at all the way Andrei eyed her, he declared publicly for all to hear, "She's my mate."

CHAPTER TWELVE

Charlotte's attention was drawn from her observation of the room to the massive man with the full beard who'd tried to squish Lawrence in a hug. The jovial fellow laughed and kept laughing. Glad someone was amused. She personally itched something fierce to leave. She was fairly certain she'd heard the word bear. Bear as in shapeshifter bears?

Where? Were there some in this very room?

She admitted to being impressed. The two-story hall was set with trestle tables and benches, the rustic look extremely well done, with aged wood tops sealed in resin. The long seating was thick and heavy to avoid toppling, but each spot had an indentation to cradle the butt.

Want something a little softer? Then adjourn to one of the spots flanking a roaring fireplace, featuring wide couches, fat armchairs, and rugs. Lots of them. Everywhere she looked, she saw even more shag carpet on the stone-paving floor.

She half expected to see candles when she looked

up; however, the owner had opted for electric lighting set in a massive wooden wheel and long-finned ceiling fans to move air around. A necessary thing given the amount of people inside. Thirty to forty at least. They appeared to have walked into a party of giants.

Or so it appeared to her given she was shorter by at least a foot, two in many cases. Outweighed as well. There was a similarity to the crowd, with most of them owning lush, dark hair. Not a bald head to be seen, and most of the men sported a full jaw of hair. The women were broad and solid looking, their laughter as bold as the men's.

Lord help her if she'd gone from being in a car full of lions to a den of bears. What was next, a pit of crocodiles?

I have to get out of here. Escape before she was well and truly screwed, but how? To return to civilization she'd need to steal a car at the very least. Steal from lions and giants and bears.

Oh my.

But what was the alternative?

The massive man bore down on her, wearing a determined grin, but Lawrence beat him, sweeping an arm around her waist before she could protest.

"Peanut, my dear mate, I'd like you to meet my old friend, Andrei," Lawrence announced rather loudly.

His mate? She cocked him a glance, and he gave a quick tilt of his head that said, *Play along?*

"You actually did it?" Andrei sounded more surprised than anything. "You silly bastard." More laughter erupted, which meant she wasn't paying attention as he added, "Let me hug the bride."

Wait, he was talking about—

"Eep!" Charlotte couldn't help the squeak as she was grabbed. For a second, Lawrence's arm tightened, and she feared being caught in a tug of war that might hurt.

"Two seconds. No longer," he said as he released her.

Andrei—who looked nothing like the wrestling giant —engulfed her in a hug that would surely break every bone in her body. The man smelled surprisingly good and proved quite gentle, meaning she was quite all right when he set her back down on her feet.

A possessive arm claimed her waist, and she allowed it. Even leaned into it.

"I can't believe you got mated." Andrei shook his head. "I never thought you'd ever settle down."

"It only takes the right person," Lawrence lied smoothly.

He had to be because he couldn't seriously think that. They barely knew each other. This had to all be an act.

"I thought all the children were in bed." The remark came from a rather tall lady wearing her dark hair in ringlets around her head.

It was meant to antagonize Charlotte, and it worked. But she couldn't let it show. "I look young for my age."

"It's your size. You're awfully small." A sly gaze slid past Charlotte onto Lawrence. "And didn't I hear you say she's your mate? An odd pairing. Aren't you afraid she'll break if you're too vigorous? We both know how you like it rough."

The implication proved less than subtle, and Lawrence stiffened, his fingers digging in before he removed them entirely. "Lada, as classy as ever, I see." Lawrence looked ill-pleased.

"Since when do you want a lady?"

"Since he decided he was done sleeping with trash," was Charlotte's blurted retort.

It widened a few sets of eyes and then narrowed Lada's in fury. "Are you insulting me?"

"If you can't tell, does it count?" Charlotte couldn't help herself. Her mouth ran and got her into deeper trouble. Just making friends everywhere she went. Not.

Andrei broke the tension. "Your mate has a bit of fire in her. You just need to fatten her up."

"Charlotte is perfect as she is," was Lawrence's reply, and it warmed her.

Yes, it might be a lie, an act for these bold people, but she enjoyed it. For about five seconds.

"Are you drunk?" Lada exclaimed. "Perfect how? Have you seen her? Undersized and *human*."

The insult proved blatant and rude. It also assumed Charlotte would stand there and take it. Listen to a jealous sow. Yes, jealous because someone couldn't hold on to her man.

It brought out the shit disturber in her. Despite Lawrence having moved slightly apart from her, she tucked in close. His arm slid right around her as if it belonged.

She smiled at Lada. "Don't worry about my sweet Roarie. My cuddly kitty is more than satisfied with what I have to offer. Why, we just came back from a lovely unplugged vacation in the wilderness. Just me, him, and a fireplace. Pity his aunts can't leave him alone for more than a few days or we'd still be there, naked in front of that fire."

Lawrence's face suddenly ended up buried in her hair, and she'd have sworn he slightly shook.

Lada's lips pressed tight. "Better enjoy it while you can. It won't last. It never does."

"Are you sure about that? I hear being mated is a permanent thing." She angled her neck to show off her marks, and Lada's face turned red.

"I need a drink." Lada whirled and stomped off.

A slow clap led to Andrei laughing. "Fuck me on top of the dryer on tumble, it's not often Lada is put in her place."

But she'd only won against Lada because she'd lied. She'd pretended the whole mating thing was real. As if. While Lawrence might no longer be a complete stranger, she remained unready to call him husband. And from the sounds of it, he wasn't the type to tie himself to one woman.

It meant sooner rather than later this charade would end. But until it did, she had to play a role. Right now, that was pretending to be his lovey-dovey wife. Or mate, as they kept calling her.

He seemed especially interested in making sure he shoved that fact in Andrei's face. The big man, to his credit, let all the jibes roll right off him, usually laughing and giving it back just as good.

Lawrence made the comment of, "Judging by the

pounds you've packed on, you must be ready to hibernate."

"Not all of us like to be as skinny as a prepubescent boy. I am all man." A remark served with a wink in her direction.

It didn't mean a thing. She could see Andrei did it on purpose, and yet Lawrence acted as if he were annoyed. Dare she even say jealous? Over her?

Should she be flattered he showed such ardent interest? It certainly warmed her in some interesting places. Or should she be insulted that he thought she'd be so shallow as to let him touch her one minute and then, right in front of him, make plans for seduction with someone else?

It was so utterly strange and different that she decided to enjoy it. Why not? This charade would end in another day. Two at the most. She snuggled by his side as they filled a plate high with food and shared it. Utensils appeared to be lacking, so everyone ate with their fingers. Lawrence fed her, dabbing chunks of hot bread into whipped butter. She might have moaned at the simple pure pleasure of the taste.

He looked pained.

She put a hand on his arm as he looked away. "Are you okay?"

"Fine. Just fine."

"Are you sure? Maybe you should lie down."

"Maybe I should," he mumbled.

"What's this? Is my little liger tired already? Getting too old to hang with the men?" Andrei taunted.

The challenge tightened Lawrence's lips. In another

second the testosterone dicks would really start swinging. She needed a way to get them out of here that left him with his pride. Only one thing would shut Andrei up.

She smiled and leaned forward, knowing her blouse with its missing button gaped. Something their host noticed. When she'd first arrived, she had worried about the fact she'd not properly bathed in days, only to realize no one cared. It also helped Andrei had the happy face of a man well into his cups. In this case, liter-sized mugs that he kept refilling.

His gaze followed the dark crevice as she murmured, "Don't be silly. My cuddly Roarie isn't tired. It's our code for, 'Let's ditch everyone and find a place we can be alone.'"

"Make him wait. Stay here, drink more with me, and drive him completely mad," Andrei suggested with a raised rakish brow.

Her lips tilted. "What makes you think it wouldn't make me just as insane? We are, after all, still newly mated." She put her hand on Lawrence's, and his fingers laced with hers.

"Ah, young love." Andrei sighed. "Far be it from me to get in its way. Still, the night is young and full of bears."

"Isn't the expression beers?" she replied.

"My mistake." Andrei tilted his head and stared at her while talking to Lawrence. "She has no idea, does she?" A cryptic statement.

"She knows enough."

"Which is too much." Andrei drummed his fingers. "You put me in a difficult spot."

"Leave her alone, Andrei." Lawrence barely spoke above a whisper, and yet there was a vibrating strength to the demand.

But the bigger concern? Why did Lawrence think Andrei threatened her?

"If it isn't chubby Andrei. Look at you all grown up. And that cute peach fuzz of a beard." Aunt Lacey was the one to suddenly appear between the men, smiling widely, and ruffling Andrei's hair. "I see someone's been eating his breakfast and those of his brothers."

"Lacey. You look ravishing."

"And you are quite drunk, which is impressive for a bear. What do you say we leave my nephew and share a few toasts?" Lacey winked.

Was she really flirting with the younger man?

"How about we crack a keg I've been saving?" Andrei stood and slung an arm around Lacey before they headed away.

Aunt Lenore took her place, snapping her fingers. "Let's go while she's got him distracted. You just had to antagonize him."

"Me? He practically propositioned Charlotte," Lawrence said.

"Is she not capable of saying no herself?" asked his aunt.

To which she replied, "I did. But he's a man, which means the potential for stupid—"

"Is multiplied!" Lena exclaimed, arriving at the rear. "Damned those giant bastards. I swear the Medvedev are always looking for trouble."

"You know that, yet brought us here anyhow."

Lawrence held her hand as they escaped the big room for a hallway and, at the far end, stairs.

"We came because they have really good mead. We will drive home in the morning after a decent night's rest."

He snorted. "Like you party cats are going to sleep."

Pretending affront, Lenore sniffed. "I feel so attacked."

That brought a smile to Charlotte's lips.

Lenore swept open a door two flights and three halls later. "While you were pissing off Andrei, I had some rooms assigned to us."

"Not my fault he was already drunk," Lawrence grumbled.

"They're having quite the party," Charlotte observed.

"That's their nightly routine," Lena scoffed. "You want to see a real party? Come for the winter and summer solstice. It has five times as many people and lasts for days."

"Even so, make sure to lock the door. Sometimes Andrei and his family like to wander," was Lena's reminder.

The aunts were gone before Charlotte had time to realize it was her and Lawrence alone, in a room with one bed. "We're sharing a room?"

"We're mated. It's kind of expected."

"Oh." It didn't occur to her they'd keep playing at the role outside of the public eye.

"My aunt just told you. Old rivalry."

She shook her head. "It's more than that with the pair of you."

"You've met him, right?"

"I have, and he's big, loud, boisterous, and seems to genuinely like you for some reason despite the fact you're an ass."

"I thought you understood he's a bear."

"For real? I thought you were maybe joking."

"Why would I make it up?" He sounded confused.

"Was everyone downstairs a bear?"

"No."

She sighed and then clenched as he added,

"Pretty sure there were at least two wolves, too."

"Why do you hate Andrei in particular?"

"Lions and bears don't get along."

She got the impression it was more than that. "Your aunts seem okay with them. And I'm going to go out on a limb and say you liked Lada a little too much one night."

He grimaced. "I didn't mean to. Remember that mead my aunt says is so good? It's potent. I got drunk with Andrei, and I woke up to her on top. No idea how she got there, but I was young. Dumb. I didn't tell her to get off. And she's been clingy ever since."

It was brutally explicit, and Charlotte might have been more put off but for the honesty. "I get the impression you don't like to date."

"Don't mind the dating. It's the rest that stumps me." At her blank look. he explained. "At dinner, I saw you preferred the red wine to the white, and between the two reds you tried, you chose the dark label over the pink stuff."

"What's my preference in wines have to do with anything?"

"It's got to do with taste. To find out what you liked, you tried a couple of vintages. Probably enjoyed a few before settling on a favorite. Yet even a favorite pales over time, so you go back to trying more, looking for the next wine that quenches your thirst."

"Am I understanding this right? You're comparing all the women you meet to crappy wines you don't want to drink?"

"Why force yourself to like something? Shouldn't the wine you settle on be perfect? Just like the partner you settle on should tick every box."

"And you've never met someone who came close?"

He opened his mouth, and she expected him to say no. "Not until now."

She blinked at the allusion. Heat curled in her chest. She was elated by the statement; however, it seemed too perfect. She didn't buy it. "Is this your dorky-ass way of saying it's different with me? Let me guess, I'm like the champagne of all wines. Since you've met me, I'm the only thing you want to drink."

"Something like that."

She snorted. "Puh-lease. I am not that gullible."

"What makes you think I'm lying?"

"Because it's been like what, three days since we met? Most of that a high-stress situation. Meaning you don't know the real me. The one who likes to sit around in pajamas on weekends and eat frozen dinners and do puzzles while binging Netflix."

"Add a roaring fire and that sounds like perfection."

"You think it sounds romantic? It's not."

"Actually, it sounds relaxing and comfortable. Which I'm totally for."

"Stop trying to pretend this mating thing is going to work. Whatever you think you're feeling right now isn't authentic. Once we get back to normal life, you'll realize I'm not the wife you're looking for."

"What if you are?"

"Why are you being so stubborn about this? And don't tell me it's because of the bite. Would you feel better if I wore a scarf and hid it?"

"No!"

"You can't base your life off some silly ritual. Like you said before, I'm human. Surely any weird cat rules you have don't apply to me."

His jaw locked. His body tensed with anger. "You want to leave me."

"Can you really blame me? Shit hasn't exactly been sane since we met."

He scrubbed a hand through his hair. "I know. And I'm sorry for that. I didn't exactly plan this. Definitely never expected you."

"Ouch."

He whirled. "That wasn't meant as an insult. Just that you were a surprise."

"Like a puck to the teeth."

His turn to wince. "It wasn't that bad."

"But it wasn't something you wanted. What do you want from me?" she asked. "Because one minute you're like together forever, and the next you're a man whore who will never settle down."

"How about I'm a man who wants a happily ever after but is worried he's too much of a whore to settle down?"

"That's what I just said."

"Which just goes to show you how confused I am. I don't know what's happening between us. It's new for me, too. All I can say is there is something about you. I crave you, not just your body but your presence, your voice. And when you touch me..." He purred, and his gaze dropped to her mouth.

The words were pure seduction, and they fluttered over her flesh, tightening her breasts, clenching her pelvis. "Sounds more like a case of blue balls on account we were interrupted. You'd probably feel different if we'd had sex."

His lips quirked. "That is a possibility. And one we could fix." He glanced at the bed. The only bed.

She understood what he suggested. Sex. With him.

And she was tempted. So damned tempted. But she'd spent the last few days working in a kitchen, being kidnapped—not once but twice—and hadn't had a shower in as many days. Although she'd managed to sneak a number two earlier when she'd left during dinner to find a washroom.

"Let me think about it."

He yawned rather than argue. "I don't know about you, but I am looking forward to a night in a real bed."

The only bed drew her gaze. Surely it was big enough to handle them both because she wasn't about to eschew the bed for her flimsy morals.

"Think they left us any jammies?" she asked.

He shook his head and pulled off his shirt. "Doubtful. Bears are even bigger nudists than lions. I'm surprised they were all dressed downstairs. Although, given the keg they rolled out, give it another hour and that will probably change."

"Your aunts..."

"Will probably start the strip poker game."

Her nose wrinkled. "Your family is weird."

"Yeah."

She softened her words with, "But they really love you."

"Yeah." He offered a small smile as his fingers went to the waistband of his trackpants.

She turned, cheeks flaming. It wasn't as if she'd not seen it, but now was different.

Much of her anger had faded. She was out of the woods. Safe. Being flirted with by the most gorgeous man. And now she knew what that man could make her body feel. Was it any wonder she tingled between the legs?

"Come to bed, Peanut."

"I need to shower first." She fled him for the chilly washroom with its ornate vanity, bowl sink, toilet with bidet—including a hot air blower she'd experienced on the main floor. No toilet paper here. And a big, multi-head shower with a glass partition and a pebbled bottom that also had a dark line of stone that waved up the white subway tile. The water took only seconds to jet out hot.

She stepped into it and sighed. Heaven. Pure. Freaking pleasure.

The glass wall steamed up, and she lifted her face

into the spray. Groaned. Then gasped as hands slid around her.

"Lawrence?" She whirled and found him behind her in the shower. "What are you doing?"

"Hopefully helping you shower. Or do you want me to leave?"

If he hadn't given her a choice, if he'd said something cocky, she might have been able to say no. But he held himself still. Waited for a reply.

She cupped his cheek, drew him down for a kiss, and whispered, "I think the shower is big enough for two."

He groaned as he lifted her off her feet and moved them until her back pressed against the cold tile, drawing a sharp inhale. His lips caught the sound in a torrential kiss, and she was just fine with that. With this.

She wanted him. And right now, in this moment, he wanted her.

Despite the frantic nature of the kiss, he eventually slowed, taking his time. He set her down slowly, even leaning his body slightly away from her that he might stroke his hands up and down her frame. He touched her lightly, tickling fingers over her ribs then down her side, following the slight swell of her waist and hips before dipping lower to cup her full bottom.

He pulled her tight to him. The hardness of his cock became trapped against her lower belly. So hard. For her. A desire both flattering and exciting.

His fingers threaded through her hair, angling her head as he took his time tasting her lips. The sensuality of it drew a trembling shiver. The slight motion enough to rub her nipples over his chest. They turned into hard buds that scraped his flesh, and he stilled.

The kiss stopped but only because he had another use for his mouth. Soft nibbles trailed down her neck. She shivered and arched as his lips moved lower, the scruffy beginnings of a beard abrading her skin in a good way. The hands cupping her bottom slid up her ribcage until they hefted her breasts.

He palmed them, squeezed them, pushed them together to rub his face in the crease. The tease had her wet and squirming.

She reached for him, but he shifted his hips. "Don't."

"Why not?" she grumbled as he kept sucking at her nipples, each tug a pleasurable jolt.

"Because I don't want this to be over yet, and if you touch me..." He didn't need to finish. The arousal at his words flushed her head to toe.

He growled against the flesh in his mouth, vibrating the bud, and she moaned. She threaded her fingers through his damp strands of hair and held tight as he suckled her nipples, nibbling and teasing each one in turn until she finally had to beg.

"Lawrence, please."

"As you command."

She had no breath to protest when, instead of giving her his cock, he dropped to his knees. His lips found her thighs and pressed scalding brands on her flesh. He ran a finger along the part of her legs, and she spread them. He rewarded her with a stroke over her lips.

Teasing her with a simple touch, he leaned forward and nuzzled her pubes, even as his fingers returned to drag across the swollen lips of her sex. Back and forth, and her focus was so intent he had to remind her, "Breathe, Peanut, or better yet, scream for me," he said before he placed his mouth on her.

Oh. My. Ohhh. Moans slipped from her as he lapped at her, his tongue quick and sure, the strokes just right as they lavished attention on her clitoris. When she thought she'd explode, he'd sense it and dip for a taste between her lips. Just as decadent and she clutched at him, gripping his wet head tight, mostly so she wouldn't fall down because her legs had turned to jelly.

As if sensing her pleasurable dilemma, his hands gripped her hips, which not only helped keep her upright but allowed a better angle to lick with his tongue. And when he tugged her clit with his lips?

She couldn't hold on anymore. With a cry, she burst, her climax rushing through her, making her throb and gasp and shudder. But he wasn't done. He stood, and with one hand lifting her leg to angle it around his hip, he spread her wide for the thrust of his cock.

He filled her perfectly, his cock thick and long, curved just the right way so that each stroke hit her in that special spot. With only a few thrusts, he brought her waning climax back to life. He hit her G-spot over and over, drawing short bursts of air from her. She clung to him, and when his lips sought hers, their kiss was more just a way of meshing even closer.

His hips kept thrusting, and she felt it build then peak, the muscles of her channel clenching even tighter during this second orgasm. So tight he gasped.

When the climax finally ebbed, she was boneless

jelly. He was the one to help soap and rinse her. He was the one to wrap her in a big fluffy towel and then carry her to bed.

She woke in the morning with him spooned around her, the hot length of his cock throbbing against her backside.

"Morning, Peanut," he murmured against her hair.

"Mornin'." She couldn't exactly blush given what they'd done, and yet she felt awkward.

Not Lawrence. "We have time before breakfast." He wiggled against her.

"There better still be bacon."

"I'll give you something salty," he growled into her ear.

By the time he slid into her she was panting and writhing.

For a girl who usually didn't like morning sex, she came so hard she soaked the bed.

CHAPTER THIRTEEN

C harlotte wouldn't come out of the bathroom, and
Lawrence couldn't figure out why.

"Peanut, what's wrong?"

"Go away."

"Not until you tell me why you ran in there and
locked the door."

"Isn't it obvious?"

"Would I be asking otherwise?" Because that seemed
much more obvious to him.

"I'm sorry about the bed."

"What about it?"

"It's wet," was her horrified whisper.

He grinned. "Yes. Yes, it is." He'd never felt anything
more glorious than her gushing over his buried cock.

"I didn't mean to pee."

Only then did he realize she misunderstood what
had happened. "Not pee. You're a gusher, Peanut. You
came so hard, you *came*."

"Gross. Erg." He heard the creak of the door as she

slumped against it. "Gushing is something those Juicy Squirt candies do. Not me."

"Because you'd not met the right man."

"Don't you dare make this a cocky, I'm-so-good-at-sex kind of thing."

"Would you feel better if I said you're the first woman I've ever made gush? And I've never been more flattered."

She opened the door a crack and peeked. "I couldn't help myself. It was..."

"The best sex you ever had. You're welcome."

Her nose wrinkled. "Thanks for reminding me you're a slut."

"Shaming me?" He arched a brow.

"Making an observation."

"All before I met you."

"You expect me to believe that you're suddenly a one-woman kind of man?" The door opened wider. "Please. I'm not that gullible."

"Why not?"

"Because you'll get bored of me. I'm not a lion or a bear. Or anything interesting. I'm just me."

"Exactly."

She rolled her eyes. "You already had sex with me. You don't need to butter me up."

"I see we're going to have to work on the trust issue."

"There is no trust issue because there is no we."

"If you say so, Peanut." But he wasn't as sure as her. While he had his doubts about the mate thing, he could admit one thing at least. He wasn't bored yet.

"What do you say we find some food? I am starved."

There were a lot of hungover faces at breakfast. Not his aunts of course. They could drink even any man, or woman, under a table.

It was as he finished eating that he asked his aunts, "When do we leave?"

"We're not going yet, but you can take the car if you want," Lenore offered, working on her second plate of pancakes.

"You're staying? Why?"

"Unfinished business." Lenore winked at some fellow across the hall. He blanched.

Lawrence might have argued, but if they didn't want to come then that meant more time alone for him and Charlotte. Time to connect, only she wasn't saying much. They had nothing to pack and were soon on their way.

With each mile, she grew more withdrawn, but it wasn't until they reached the city outskirts that he found out why.

"Where are you going?" she asked.

"My hotel."

"Do you mind dropping me off at my apartment first?"

"I'm afraid I can't do that."

"Why?"

"For one, there are bad guys after us."

"Us. Or you?"

"Even if they have given up, there's an even bigger reason for us to stay together. Or have you forgotten what I told you about that mark on your neck?" She might not be taking the mate bond seriously, but for him, the conviction this was real only got stronger.

She groaned. "Not the damn bite thing again. You bit me. We had sex. It's done. We both know this isn't going anywhere."

"Are you sure about that?" All he had to do was put his hand lightly on her thigh to feel her shiver.

"So what if we're still attracted to each other? Big deal. If you want, we can hook up again before I leave."

"Leave? Where are you going?"

"Home. Back to America."

"What about finding your brother?"

"It's time I gave up. I have no more money. No leads. Nothing. I'm wasting my time here."

"I told you I'd help."

"Help how? It's been months since he disappeared, and I've gotten nothing in all that time."

"I have access to more channels than you. Give me a few days, and I'll have information for you."

"Don't. Just leave it alone."

It was only by some strange perception that he guessed her fear. "You think if we go looking for Peter, we'll find out he's dead."

She flinched. "Right now, I can still pretend he's alive and just missing. I can have some hope." Her lips trembled.

"Ah, Peanut." He wanted to hold her something fierce, but she remained withdrawn. Not the wanton woman he'd made come so hard just that morning.

"I don't want your pity."

"It's called commiseration."

"Whatever. You need to turn at the next street for my apartment."

"We're going to my hotel."

"I told you—"

He cut her off. "In case you've forgotten, we were kidnapped a few days ago."

"*You* were. I was just an accident of timing."

"Were you? It occurs to me that I might not have been the man they were looking for."

"What are you talking about?" Said much too quickly.

"Don't play stupid. What if none of this was about me after all, and I was the accident in timing?"

"You're the one who declared they were after you."

"A valid assumption given I have a tendency of pissing people off, but in retrospect, I might have been wrong. No one ever asked me my name. Which leads me to wonder, what if I was never their target? But you were. What kind of business would you say your bother is involved in?" Her lips pressed into a line, and he had his answer. "Let's hypothesize for a second. Let's say those people were looking for your brother. That would mean he's not dead but hiding."

"Then isn't it better if we leave him alone until the bad guys stop looking? What if we lead them right to him?"

"What if he needs our help?"

She chewed her lower lip, making him very jealous. "If he's in that kind of trouble, then I should be going to the police."

"You want to call the Russian police?" He arched a brow. "So you want him to go to jail?"

The sigh was long and loud. "What do you suggest I do?"

"Let me put out some feelers, see if people in my network might have heard or seen him. At the same time, I can find out more about those people who kidnapped us. See if it's your brother they wanted and, if so, what they were trying to extort from him."

"Can't be money. He's always broke, and I doubt he's got any hidden treasure. I've been through his apartment. There's nothing."

"Then you won't have a problem humoring me later when I go take my own look."

"Why later? Why not go there now?"

"Because the hotel is right there." He pointed. "And it's been hours since I've made you come."

"Lawrence!" She said his name in a high pitch that had him chuckling.

"What can I say? I am addicted to you."

He pulled to a stop in front of the hotel, and a doorman approached, ready to help her out. Lawrence moved fast enough to intercept him, skimming over the hood of the car, hitting the other side in time to hip check the doorman, open the door, and hold out his hand to her.

She eyed it and him before grasping it. He hauled her out and held her close a moment longer than necessary.

"Did you really have to knock him down for trying to do his job?"

"Yes." His grin was unrepentant.

"You're bad."

"The worst," he agreed.

She swayed on her feet, looking exhausted.

"Do you want me to carry you?"

She shook her head. "What would people say?"

"I should probably mention that the hotel is paid handsomely to look the other way."

"More of your secrets," she mumbled.

"Not for much longer. Give me a chance and I'll fill you in on what I can."

"What if I don't want to know?"

"Would you rather I kept quiet?"

She pressed her lips. "I'm too tired to think. Ask me again tomorrow."

She fell into step with him, only stiffening as they passed the doormen. To their credit, they held open the portals without a world despite their wretched appearance.

There weren't many people around, which proved lucky. They made it to his suite without seeing anyone else. He immediately kicked off his shoes and headed for the mini bar. She remained frozen by the door.

"Don't stand there. Get comfortable. If you want a shower, there's a robe in the bathroom."

"A shower sounds nice."

"As hot and long as you like, Peanut."

Magic words that finally brought a smile. "You might regret that."

He did, but only because she spent a long time in there alone. Naked. Whereas he made do with the second smaller bathroom with its simple shower. But it did the job, and he resisted the temptation to join her.

It was torture, but he wanted her to relax. She was exhausted. Wary around him. He was also curious to see what would happen if he didn't make the first move.

When she emerged, swaddled in white terry cloth, her hair bound in a towel, her glasses crooked, it was to find him lounging on the sofa, phone in hand. He'd had the front desk send up a replacement and now went through some text messages. Most of them assuming he'd gone on a bender or was hiding from an irate father/husband again. Did people really think so little of him?

"How are you feeling?"

"Human again."

He snorted. "Was that meant to be a bad joke?"

"I forgot about the pussy cat thing. Do you even have showers or baths or do you just lick yourself clean?" she asked, her eyes twinkling with mirth.

"Just for that maybe I won't give you the clothes I ordered. You look better out of them anyhow."

"Lawrence!"

"It's the truth." He loved the blush on her cheeks.

"What smells so good?" she asked, clutching the neck of her robe tight. The modesty amused, given he'd licked most of those intimate inches.

"I had some food brought up."

The joy in her expression made him wish it weren't for edibles.

"Where?"

He stood, but before he could point, she practically ran for the trolley and its covered plates. She snared one heaped with chicken, potatoes, and some kind of creamy sauce served with a vegetable. She used a bun to sop at the juice and devoured it.

He ate as well, quiet, waiting for her to lead the conversation because he wasn't sure how to start. It wasn't until she'd groaned her way through dessert—a frothy concoction laced with sugar and fruit—that she finally found her tongue.

"That was good."

"Only good?"

"I kind of missed eating with our fingers." Her gaze went to them, and he hardened.

Was she also remembering what else those fingers had done? The feel of his mouth on her flesh? "I'm still hungry."

"I don't think there's anything left." She glanced at the table then him.

"Never said I was hungry for food."

She inhaled sharply.

"I guess the question is, am I bad at it?" He arched a brow, a light tease to soften the moment. "You did, after all, claim the reason I never got seconds was because I possibly failed as a lover."

The reminder brought a smirk. "Are you still miffed about that? Do you need me to say you were adequate?"

"Adequate?"

"Fine, not bad."

"You're killing me here, Peanut."

"Would you prefer I tell you that being with you is like being tossed in a storm and emerging from the other side feeling as if you've been wrung dry?"

He stared at her. "Meaning I do suck at it."

She laughed. "On the contrary, you are much too good. Good enough that I can't help myself." She rose and, biting her lower lip, moved until she stood in front of him. Her cheeks flamed as she said, "Weren't you the one who said he was too impatient to take me home?"

"Is that a complaint?"

"Just wondering if you're a man of your word."

"Sit on my lap and I'll show you."

She straddled him. Her robe split apart, meaning he was inside her within seconds. She rode him, her fingers gripping the chair back, her head leaning back, her wet hair dangling, her body writhing atop him.

He did his best to rock with her, his flesh squeezed and heated, her flesh welcoming. When she came, he couldn't help but come with her.

The pleasure was intense. And already he craved it again. But it could wait until they'd rested was his final thought as she fell asleep in his arms.

CHAPTER FOURTEEN

W hy did it have to feel so good?

That was Charlotte's one regret as she snuck out of the bed with the large sprawled man. Her lover. And according to him, his mate.

It would be easy and pleasurable to take what he offered. To enjoy the sex. The attention. The feeling that she wasn't just worthy but loved.

However, she didn't need a crystal ball to see they were doomed. Not just because he was a lion and much too pretty for her.

Everyone kept telling her he wasn't the type to be satisfied with one woman forever, and she wasn't foolish enough to believe for one second she could be that woman if such a one existed. Problem being, if she stayed with him, she might start hoping. Already a part of her fluttered whenever he looked at her with that soft expression of his. She craved his touch.

Best to leave now while she could resist the temptation.

Just one problem.

Lawrence caught her as she was about to open the hotel room door. "Where are you going?"

She wrinkled her nose. She'd hoped to avoid a confrontation. "Leaving, obviously."

"And you've obviously thought this through. Because the first thing I'm wondering is, what will you do without a wallet or any money?"

"Bum a ride." Which was admittedly the biggest flaw in her plan.

"Bum a ride from a stranger instead of waking me? Are you that desperate to escape?"

Yes, because the more time she spent with him, the more she downplayed all the reasons why she shouldn't get involved. "It's been fun, but you have your own life. I have mine." Kind of.

"You can't just walk away, Peanut. We have unfinished business."

"Watch me." She opened the door but failed to walk out as the aunts blocked the door.

"You ain't going anywhere," Lena drawled, pushing her way inside.

"You can't stop me."

Lacey sounded almost apologetic as she said, "Sorry, dearie, but in this case, she's absolutely correct. We can't allow you to leave."

"Excuse me? It's not up to you."

"Actually, it is. Pride security," Lenore declared with a snap of her fingers. "Which means we decide who poses a security threat."

"What threat? You're like twice my size," Charlotte retorted.

"That's just mean," Lenore declared hotly.

Lena, the last one to enter, added, "Not Lenore's fault she has no will power around the dessert bar."

"You're one to talk."

"Some of us work out." Lena flexed.

Lenore laughed. "Settle it with an arm wrestle?"

"Can you do that later?" Lacey huffed. "We left a perfectly warm den because of the Charlotte problem."

"Ah yes, our nephew's supposed mate."

"No supposed about it," he said from the spot he'd commandeered on the suite's couch. "She is mine."

"Looks to me like she's having issues with it," Lenore pointed out.

"Then she needs to deal with it," Lena barked.

As if she would be cowed by something this important. "Excuse me, but this is my life you're trying to manipulate. I never agreed to marry your nephew. And if you find me difficult now, see what happens if you try to make me a prisoner."

"We don't have much of a choice," Lenore observed, flopping down beside Lawrence. "Here's the facts. You are in the possession of a certain secret that is very important to us. The only reason you're still alive is because Roarie wouldn't like it if we killed you."

"Killed me? What the hell is wrong with you?" Charlotte exclaimed. She whirled on Lawrence. "Are you going to let her talk to me like that?"

"No one is killing you."

Her lips pursed. "I won't be a prisoner."

"Then do something about it!" snapped Lena. "Don't you look at my nephew and expect him to save you. Save yourself."

Charlotte's gaze narrowed. "I tried that. You wouldn't let me leave."

"Because you need to prove you're not a threat."

"How can I do that if you've got me locked up?" was her exasperated argument.

"She's got a point," Lawrence observed. He leaned over the coffee table, lit with a menu screen that he was making choices from.

"Ooh if you're ordering breakfast, I need some protein. Eggs. Bacon. Sausage. Ham." Lenore ticked off the items. "No hash browns, though. I'm watching the carbs."

"Pastries for me, because some of us don't have that issue." Lacey smirked.

"Order your own breakfast, in your room," Lawrence ordered. "This is for me and Peanut only."

"We can't leave. She's a security risk to the Pride, meaning she can't stray from our sight."

"You've got to be kidding," Charlotte breathed. "You can't stalk me."

"We will," was Lena's grim proclamation.

"Until we know we can trust you," Lacey added with an apologetic shrug.

"Lawrence?" She turned a questioning gaze on him.

"Yeah, Lawrence, what you going to do?" taunted Lenore.

He rubbed the spot between his eyebrows. "Can this wait until after I've eaten?"

"I think we just got your answer," was Charlotte's cold reply. She moved for the door, determined to leave. Would they dare lay hands on her?

Lacey tried to get in her way. "Sorry, but you can't go."

It was Lena grabbing her arm that made Charlotte snap. "Let go of me."

Her sharp rebuke had Lawrence growling. "Unhand her."

"I will when she behaves."

"Now." A single menacing syllable that exhaled as he rose from the couch.

His aunt Lena arched a brow but loosened her grip on Charlotte. "Did you really just sass me?"

"No one touches my mate."

"It's our job to protect the Pride. She's a threat," Lenore pointed out.

"I'm not going to tell anyone." No one would believe her.

"Says you. But then one night you get drunk and start blabbing..." Lena pinched her fingers and thumb, making her hand into a talking mouth. "Then people start theorizing, then we have to pull a few Epsteins..." She shook her head. "When it can all be avoided, right here, right now."

The chill in her body was chased as Lawrence drew close. He didn't touch her, and yet his warmth penetrated. She stepped back against him, unconsciously seeking the closeness. His arm went around her upper body, and he palmed her belly, fingers lightly curled around her waist.

His voice emerged as a low rumble. "Enough of the threats. Charlotte is none of your concern."

"You made it our concern when you accidentally mated her." Lenore jabbed her finger, but it never got close. He was a shield against the wrath of his aunts.

"What if it wasn't an accident? Isn't the whole purpose of the mating bond finding the right one?"

"It is. And yet the girl hates you."

"I don't hate him," Charlotte retorted. She didn't. Her feelings for him were more complicated than that.

"But you don't want to be with him either," chided Lenore.

"Give the boy and girl a chance. It's only been a few days. They're still in the getting-to-know-each-other stage." Lacey tried to be the voice of reason. "They need to spend time together, which gives me an awesome idea. I know this great pastry shop where we could have so much fun."

Lawrence narrowed his gaze. "Is this shop in your binder?"

"Don't be silly, Roarie," Lacey batted her lashes. "As if I'd resort to a bakery so far from the event."

"What event? What binder is he talking about?" Charlotte asked, completely lost.

"Forget the binder. It's not important. After breakfast, how about you and I go to your brother's apartment?"

He'd no sooner made the offer than Lena was shaking her head, uttering a vehement, "No."

"Why not?"

"You can go after we sweep it and make sure it's clean."

"Clean of what?" Charlotte hotly queried. "How dare you imply I'm dirty!" She bristled, and his hand flattened on her belly, making her aware of him. She glanced up and over her shoulder to see him smiling as he explained.

"My aunts are worried about listening devices and surveillance."

"Oh." That made more sense. "Who would be listening?"

"Your brother's enemies. Ours. We have to be careful."

The knock at the door announced room service. Lawrence shooed them out the door while the hotel worker set the tray on the table.

The aunts tried to converge on it, but Lawrence stood in their way. "Out."

"We told you—"

"Out." He crossed his arms. "I won't ask again."

"If you're going to be that way, then fine, we'll go. For now," Lenore threatened.

Before Lena left, she jabbed Lawrence in the chest. "We will trust her in your care, but the minute she opens her mouth and tries to tell anyone..." She dragged a finger over her throat.

"Love you, too, Auntie," Charlotte sang.

"Did she just sass me?" Lena exclaimed. She went marching back in, but Lawrence sidestepped, blocking her.

"Let's all have breakfast. I'm sure everyone will feel a little better after some food."

The bacon sure did help with Charlotte's humor, especially since she waved goodbye with a piece. It meant she caught Lacey's assessing stare and could have sworn she heard the word "veil" muttered.

Such an odd trio. Bloodthirsty, too. Which was why the moment the door closed, and they were alone, she asked, "Would they really kill me?"

"In a half-second."

"Seriously?" she huffed. "And you'd let them?"

"There is no letting them do anything. My aunts are free to do and think what they want."

"Even if it involves killing me?"

"They can try. I didn't say they'd succeed." He sat in a chair right next to hers, eschewing the spot across from her to be close enough to drop a hand on her thigh. A sign of affection or possession? A little bit of both that she didn't mind.

"They hate me."

"Totally understandable. I mean you are mated to their favorite nephew."

"Meaning if I mess things up with you, I'm screwed."

"Stop worrying about them."

"Says the guy who wasn't threatened."

"Listen, if they wanted you dead, you'd already be buried in an unmarked grave somewhere."

"Not reassuring," she snapped.

"What do you want me to say? They're protective."

"They're psychopaths."

"Not entirely. They do have empathy and care for

people, but they also can be quite remorseless when it comes to protecting those they love."

"Meaning you're okay with their behavior." How could he condone their words and actions?

"Not exactly, but at the same time, they're hard to stop once they set their mind on something."

"What will you do if they come after me?"

"I won't let them kill you." He rubbed his thumb over her lower lip.

"That's not an answer."

He sighed. "Because it's complicated. They're my only family. They raised me when my parents died."

"And haven't realized yet you're a grown man."

"It's not just about me. It's about the Pride."

"The what?" They'd said something about pride before, but she got the impression it wasn't the kind she expected.

"I belong to the Pride group. My king is Arik."

"You have a lion king?" She snickered. "With a son named Simba?"

"Actually, they have a daughter named Lisa. And that's not the point. The Pride is everything, and our number one rule is we must always keep it safe."

"I can understand that, but I'm not a threat."

"Unfortunately, that's not entirely true. You became a possible threat the moment you found out about my kind."

"Then why did you tell me?" she asked.

"I didn't have a choice given my aunts showed you at the cabin."

"Why did they show me?" she asked. "I mean, if you

can smell I'm human, then why would they reveal their secret?"

He frowned. "You know what? That's a good question. Because, at the time, they didn't know we were mated. They should have been more discreet."

"Are there any other people like me?" She couldn't say human, because that would imply he wasn't. "People who know."

"Only a few non-shifters are granted that privilege. The most common reason being because of a mating."

Her hand went to her neck. "The bite is an automatic admission to the club."

"Yes and no. Usually a mating only occurs when both parties are aware and willing."

"But in my case, you bit me by accident." Her nose wrinkled. "That's kind of a dumb thing to base a marriage on. What if you chomp the wrong person?"

"I don't think it's possible to mate the wrong person."

"That would imply you don't have any divorces."

"Not when it's a true mating."

"So everyone who gets bitten gets to live happily ever after? No way. I don't believe you." She shook her head. It didn't make sense. Love. Respect. All the things that went into making a good relationship couldn't be determined with saliva in an open wound. That was just nuts.

"You can choose not to believe all you want. It doesn't change the facts. We are mated. For life. Together forever."

She scowled. "This isn't funny."

"Do I look amused?"

"I don't want to be mated to you or anyone. I want to

go home. Alone. I promise not to tell anyone about you or your aunts. As if anyone would believe me."

"Are you really sure you want to go?"

She opened her mouth to say yes, only he looked awfully cute and rumpled. "I am not ready to just start living with you on account of some weird cult rules you have."

His lips twitched. "Hardly a cult."

"I'm the type of person who needs her space. I can't be with you twenty-four seven. And I'm sure you can't either. We'd probably end up trying to kill each other."

"I agree. Which is why I'm going to ignore my aunts. You can return to your brother's apartment."

"I can?"

"But only if you'll promise to have dinner with me."

"Only dinner?" She was the one to tease for once.

"Dinner, dessert, snack, breakfast the next morning. I want it all, Peanut, but I can wait. If it's meant to be..." He didn't finish it. Didn't have to.

"*Que sera, sera.*" A foreign expression that fit the moment.

"Give me a second to get dressed and I'll drive you home."

Put a shirt over that delectable chest? A crime. Maybe she should take one for the road. She straddled him with intent, and his smile was almost enough to make her come.

"Another ten minutes won't hurt."

"Only ten?" He arched a brow. "Challenge accepted."

That quickly she was on her back with his face

between her legs, his mouth blowing hotly. She writhed and grabbed at him, hungry for more.

And he gave it to her. Brought her to the edge and held her as she came. Just as good as the last time. So good each time, and even better there was no awkwardness after. He didn't try and avoid her. He smiled her way, patted her butt, touched her casually, drawing her in for quick kisses as they located the clothing that had gone flying and dressed.

He made it hard to remember why she wanted to leave in the first place. Why couldn't she believe in the fairytale? Could it be finally her turn for a happily ever after?

Her burgeoning hope died the moment they stepped into Peter's trashed apartment and saw the message written on the wall.

GIVE OR HE DEYE.

CHAPTER FIFTEEN

The sight of the destruction triggered Lawrence. Danger. It screamed at him to do something. He almost tossed Charlotte over his shoulder and bolted.

Deep breaths controlled him.

Barely.

The peril couldn't have been more obvious. The knowledge did things to the man that were amplified in the beast.

His mate was being threatened. Or so it seemed. The message on the wall wasn't exactly clear.

GIVE OR HE DEYE.

"It's about Peter." She stated the obvious, giving Lawrence a choice in how that conversation would go.

If he let the protective part of him take control, he'd revert to his first instinct and remove her from danger no matter her thoughts on the matter. He didn't imagine that would go well. He could already hear his aunts telling him a woman didn't need a man to save her.

He stuck to, "Yup."

"I wonder what it means." She leaned forward, head cocked, as if that would help decipher the intent of the words painted in what appeared to be mustard.

"When they say give... Any idea what that could be?"

She wrinkled her nose. "It's pretty vague."

"Yes, but we do have some clues. It's obviously a tangible item or they wouldn't have tossed the place." He swept a hand, encompassing the destruction. Ripped open cushions. Drawers torn out and dumped. Cupboards pilfered, too.

"And whatever it was, they didn't find it, or why leave a message?" She tapped her lower lip. "This has to be related to the kidnapping."

"Maybe. Or could be more than one party looking for something. Does your brother have any place he might have stashed stuff other than this apartment? Bank box? Storage unit?"

She shook her head. "None that I know of."

"In my experience, most people keep their precious treasures close in case they need to flee. Hidden compartment in furniture, loose baseboard."

"Not that I've found."

"We need to look and be sure."

"Are you suggesting we go over every inch of the floor, walls, and furniture? That will take forever."

"I've got a knack for finding hidden things." He closed and locked the door behind them.

"Kind of late for that, isn't it?" she observed sourly as she kicked at a pile of clothes then recoiled as she caught the reek of piss.

An unpleasant aroma when he wore his human shape. As his feline, smells of all kinds were fascinating.

"What are you doing?" she asked as he tugged at his shirt.

"Going to change into my liger."

"Half lion, half tiger," she muttered. "I didn't even know that was a thing."

"It's not super common. Most species are just more comfortable sticking to their own kind. But every now and then, someone who shouldn't falls in love."

"Like your parents."

"Yeah." He couldn't hold her gaze as he kept undressing and gave her the abbreviated story. "They died when I was little. Car crash. A drunk driver who'd already had his license suspended twice before."

"That's so sad." Her words emerged soft, and tears glistened.

"I don't remember much. If it weren't for pictures, I'd have no clue what they looked like." He shrugged, feeling his throat tighten in a way it hadn't in a long time. He didn't usually talk about losing his parents. "My aunts took me in when my mom's family refused. The whole intermarriage thing. They'd disowned her."

"That's horrible."

"Best thing they could have done. My aunts took real good care of me." And they'd also taken care of the drunk driver.

"They love you."

"Can you blame them? I'm adorable." He winked, trying to find a bit of his cockiness to lighten the mood.

Something about Charlotte had him revealing himself in a way that left him vulnerable.

"The only person I have is Peter. And I'm pretty sure it's the same for him. Now that's he's gone, guess it's just me." Her shoulders rounded.

"We're going to find your brother."

"I hope so. Mostly so I can throttle him for worrying me." She scrubbed at her eyes. "Then once I'm done shaking him, I will bubble wrap him and lock him up somewhere, so he stops stressing me."

"At least you want to protect him. My aunts like to drop me into danger just so they can ride to my rescue." He grimaced.

She cracked a small smile. "And then lord it over you."

"All the freaking time," he huffed. "I mean they chipped me just so they could find me whenever they wanted."

"It came in handy at the cabin."

"I'd have preferred to be left alone. With you." He winked. "I don't know about you, but this place is nasty. What do you say we find what we're looking for and get out?"

"I don't see how we're going to find it."

"Easy. My more refined sense of smell will let me sniff out any hidden spots."

"You're going to turn into a giant cat inside the apartment?"

"Think of me as a slightly larger Maine coon."

"You're bigger than me."

"I am but don't try and ride me. I'm not a horse."

"You could probably bite my head off."

"But I won't. If you want to make extra sure, rub me behind the ears. It's my sweet spot."

"Um. Okay?"

He dragged her close and kissed her. Again, and again, until she was laughing. "Stop it. Fine. I'll rub your ears."

"And my belly?"

"I am not having animal sex with you."

"Peanut! That is just wrong." He winked, and to the sound of her giggling, he morphed. The euphoria of the shift bordered on pain, but the result made him welcome it. As his liger, he was big, strong, fast. And handsome.

He hit the floor on four paws, and head-butted his mate's hand. It took her a moment before tentative fingers stroked the fur on top of his head. Best she got used to this side of him now.

On the plus side, she didn't scream, but trepidation hummed through her. A step at a time. This was all very new for her and not something he could push. She needed to accept him on her terms at her own pace.

"You're soft."

He bobbed his head.

"And not smelly."

He chuffed.

"Huge, too. Are you sure I can't ride you?" said with humor.

The only kind of riding he wanted involved her naked. That wouldn't happen in this broken place. He needed to find out if anything remained hidden and get her out of here.

Moving away from Charlotte, he took a breath. In and out through his nose, his nostrils flexing as he sifted the scents, the most pungent being the urine.

The piss split into two distinct flavors. Two people had been inside the apartment, putting their hands on everything. They'd done a thorough job. Left nothing untouched.

Lawrence did a circuit of the living area and kitchen, with a tiny window in the former. No easy escape except the door to the hall. He wandered into the bedroom, also savagely ripped apart.

Springs poked from the tears in the mattress. The pillows and their foam stuffing littered the floor. Everything from the closet was tossed to the floor, and everything on the wall had been yanked. Even a shelf had been torn from its brackets. The entire room had been ransacked, and the smells were varied, with that of his Peanut strongest. She'd been living here for months, meaning she'd imprinted the most on the space. The next strongest smell belonged to the intruders.

There was a faint fourth scent. Only here. Only one spot.

His gaze strayed upwards to the ceiling with its lazily rotating fan. He pawed a switch, and the blades slowed.

"You think he hid it in the ceiling?" she asked, craning to look upward.

He stood on the bed, the captain kind that sat upon a pair of drawers that had been yanked and turned upside down. The mattress sat at an angle, but the plywood in the frame remained, giving him a steady platform. He'd need it given the ceiling in this room sat at least nine feet.

Since he'd need hands for the next bit, he shifted just as Charlotte stepped closer, putting her eyes almost level with his junk.

He stiffened. Quite literally.

She gasped. Hotly. A sloe-eyed glance peeked at him through partially lowered lashes. The corner of her mouth lifted. "Not exactly the right time, wouldn't you say?"

"I can't help myself around you." The honest truth.

"Ditto," was her reply. Not the most sexy or romantic word and yet he hardened quite a bit more.

"Still not the right time or place," she chided.

"If you'd move away, it would be easier to control." Not something he'd ever had an issue with before. Just one more difference when it came to Charlotte.

"But not half as much fun." She blew hotly on him, and his head angled back as he resisted the temptation to ravish her.

"Killing me here, Peanut."

"Pull yourself together, Roarie."

He groaned. The nickname reminding him of his aunts. It acted like a cold shower. "Way to ruin it." He reached for the fan blades and halted their slow progression. There was a pair of tiny screws holding the casing in place. The scent belonged to someone he'd never met, and yet there was a hint of familiarity to it, making it almost certainly Peanut's brother.

He looked around for something to remove the screws. Even a butter knife would work. Then it occurred to him he didn't have time to be gentle.

Grabbing the blades, he snapped them off first, and

then he managed a good grip on the metal shell that went around the ceiling fan. He gave a few wrenches and popped the screws free as the metal holes twisted.

The moment it came off down dropped a little pouch.

Charlotte reached for it and poured the contents into her hand. She frowned. "It's a key."

Problem was, they didn't have a lock.

CHAPTER SIXTEEN

W hat did the key open? The question that plagued her as Lawrence dressed. She rolled it over and over in her head as they left the apartment. She certainly didn't have the slightest clue; however, she'd wager the person who'd left the message might. Did she have what they were looking for?

If she did, only one thing to do.

As they entered the stairwell, she said, "I am going to give them the key in exchange for Peter." Why not? It wasn't as if she cared what it unlocked.

She expected Lawrence to argue with her. To tell her it was too dangerous. She'd say she didn't have a choice, whereupon he'd offer to take her place. She'd give a token protest and then accept.

Only he didn't behave as expected. Rather than pull a sexy overprotective male bit, he wanted her to actually go through with the exchange. "Excellent plan."

"Is it, though?" She began to argue against as they headed down the three flights of stairs to the main level.

"How can I make an exchange when I don't know where to meet them?"

"We have to wait for their next move," was Lawrence's observation.

"What if I don't want to wait?" she grumbled.

"Don't worry, Peanut. I doubt it will be long." He held open the door to the sidewalk.

It wasn't until the two men wearing leather jackets and shades stepped out of the alley by the apartment that she understood.

"We're being ambushed." She glared at him. "You knew."

"Not exactly. I just recognized the scent in the alley as being the same one upstairs. Follow my lead," Lawrence ordered, "and stick close."

She might have argued but for the guns.

"Halt!" one of the armed thugs commanded.

"You find?" asked the other in a heavy accent.

Lawrence crossed his arms. "Before we begin this negotiation, where's her brother?"

"Give." The hand shoved in Lawrence's direction flexed impatiently.

As if they'd hand over their only leverage.

She peeked around his bulk. "You want it, then you bring Peter."

The man had a gap between his teeth, wide enough to shove food through, when he smiled. "Take." His gun waggled in demand.

"I don't think so." Lawrence moved quickly. His hands flinging in opposite directions, but with one purpose, grabbing the thugs and slamming them together. They groaned and clutched at their heads. Lawrence frisked the smallest one and tossed a set of keys at her. "Find their car."

"Why? Are you going to steal it?" she asked as she clutched the keys and caused some lights to flash.

"Borrow."

"Should I start it?"

"Yes, but first see if you can pop the trunk."

She peered at the fob and jabbed the tiny image. A moment later the assailants were tucked away, thumping and banging.

"Can't they pop a lever to get out?" she asked, having seen a safety video on it in college.

"I bent it."

"Oh." She glanced at the trunk. "Now what? Didn't we need them to lead us to Peter?"

"Doubtful. This vehicle has GPS."

"And you think they have their lair as their home button?" She snorted. "They can't be that dumb." She slid into the passenger seat.

He fiddled at the navigation system until it switched from Russian to English. It changed the menu buttons to something they could read. "Let's find out." Scrolling the recent addresses, he tapped them and, using a reverse search on his phone, ruled a few out right off the top. "Restaurant. Business. Another business. Apartment building. Which makes it doubtful as a place they'd be holding someone hostage. This though"—he tapped an address—"is a house just outside of the city. Let's check it out."

As they drove, she got nervous. "Maybe we should call the police now."

"That's a bad idea. If they show up and bungle things, your brother could get hurt in the crossfire."

She gnawed her lower lip. "Do you think if we show up with the key, they'll actually trade Peter for it?"

"Yes."

She sighed in relief.

"And then once they have it, they'll most likely kill you both."

"What!"

He turned a scoffing snort her way. "You don't seriously think they'd let you walk away knowing what you do."

"What happened to honor among thieves?" she grumbled.

"It doesn't exist as much as you'd think. Don't worry, Peanut. I have a plan."

"Where we don't die?" Because she was really, really wishing she'd thought longer and harder about this.

"Have you forgotten what I am?"

"No, but how is being a giant feline helpful? Going to dazzle them with your mousing skills? Create a cat's cradle with some yarn?"

"You are about to find out, Peanut."

The GPS took them to a neighborhood that was a sprawling mess of streets that meandered around executive properties. About three miles from their destination, he stopped the car.

"What are you doing?"

"Your turn to drive."

"Me?" That would require unknotting her worried hands from her lap.

"Yes, you. You need to drive the rest of the way."

"What about you? What are you going to do?"

"I'll be nearby."

"Wait, you won't be with me?"

"The plan won't work if I'm in the car. While you're distracting them in the front, I'll be sneaking in to provide backup."

Trepidation had her almost wheezing. "Maybe this isn't a good idea."

His finger lifted her chin. "If you don't want to do this, then you can stay in the car and I'll go in alone."

He gave her an out. Offered her safety. She wanted to take it, but how could she ask him to bear all the risk?

Taking a deep breath, she refused. "I can help." Even if it was just to distract them with her fear and ineptness.

"Are you sure?" he asked softly, his thumb brushing over her mouth.

"Peter is my responsibility. Not yours."

He dropped a kiss on her lips. "My brave and beautiful Peanut. I'll see you on the inside."

She only wished she had his confidence. As he got out of the car, she slid behind the wheel and then had to adjust the seat. By the time she could see over the steering wheel, there was a liger outside her window. He nuzzled the glass and winked before loping off into the night. He was kind of cute in a giant-sized kind of way.

As she eased the car into Drive, her mind went in the most inane directions, wondering if he had to get shots like a regular pet every year. Did they need flea and tick protection? What did they eat? What about the bath-room? Did his home have a kitty litter box?

Would she ever find out?

First, they had to survive the upcoming exchange.

Her hands white-knuckled the steering wheel as she approached the gate. Something by her visor flashed red and was answered by the portal. The bars cranked open, and she slid the car through.

Well, that was easier than expected. She followed a long winding drive and emerged to find a house. Castle. Whatever it was, it took up a good amount of space.

She parked by a tier of steps. When she reached the massive portal, she knocked then stood in front of it and did her best not to shake.

She almost lost it when the doors opened and she was confronted by a pair of guards holding guns. The short one with the thick mustache barked at her in Russian.

Rather than reply, she raised her hands. It didn't ease the direction of the muzzles.

There was more yelling she barely understood, and then a sudden clap of hands.

The soldiers quieted, and in the sudden silence, she heard a woman's voice. "What a lucky day. I thought we'd lost you back at the farm. But here you are. Peter's sister. We've been looking for you."

Hearing her brother's name caused her heart to stut-ter. "I don't know why you'd want to find me. I'm hardly a person of interest."

An older lady stepped into view, average height, maybe five six or seven, her features sharp and yet handsome. Her bobbed hair was very chic, as was the vest of white fur over a cream-colored blouse tucked into the same color slacks. Her red lipstick stood out in contrast. "Your brother has something I want."

"Then ask him for it."

"We've tried; however, he disappeared on us, and we've run into difficulty locating him."

"Wait, you don't have him?" Her eyes widened. "But the message on the wall—"

"Was bait to bring you to us. Let's see if your brother keeps hiding with his sister's life hanging in the balance."

"I really don't know where he is, though."

"Better hope he's keeping an eye on you then, or this will be painful for nothing."

The threat chilled Charlotte's blood. "If you let me go, I can tell you where to find the key." She hoped they didn't realize she had it in her pocket.

"Bah. What use is a key without the lock it belongs to? Or does it come with a map?"

She could have lied. Instead, she shook her head. "I don't know anything."

"Which is why we need your brother." Those perfectly red lips smirked. "For the first video we record, we'll leave your face unmarked. It will make the next one where we bruise it that much more effective."

Her blood ran cold. Then hot as she heard a roar.

It distracted the lady. She frowned and waved at her men. "Go see what that is about."

Their departure left Charlotte alone with the woman. Mob Lady had a few inches and pounds on her, but Charlotte had guts.

She threw herself on the lady, and they reeled hard into a wall. The surprise was short-lived.

"Why you..." A string of Russian followed as fingers dug into her neck, and Charlotte struggled to break free.

She managed a sloppy kick. It earned a screech as her foot connected with a sensitive shin. While Mob Lady hopped, Charlotte glanced around and saw a vase. Probably old and priceless, but her life was worth more than some pottery.

She cracked it down over the lady's head. Mob Lady dropped, leaving Charlotte staring at the body.

Oh shit. Had she killed her?

"Peanut!" She heard Lawrence's voice a moment before his naked body slammed into her and swept her into his arms.

"I hit her really hard," was all she could say.

He read her mind and then reassured her. "She's not dead."

The tension eased from her. "Oh good." She leaned into him. "And this was all for nothing. She doesn't know where Peter is. It was all a plot to use me as bait."

"As bait for what?" Lada emerged suddenly, her presence surprising. To Charlotte at least.

Lawrence acted as if he'd expected it. "Lada, what a surprise. Are you resorting to stalking these days?"

"You wish. I came to meet with my associate." Her gaze dropped to the woman on the floor.

"You know her? What is she looking for? What does she want from my brother?" Charlotte couldn't contain the questions.

"Your brother?" Lada's mouth rounded. "He's the one we've been looking for?"

"Why?" asked Lawrence.

"Wouldn't you like to know," Lada taunted.

"You will tell me." He took a menacing step forward, only to have Lada shake her head and pull a gun.

"You really should have chosen better, Law. This will hurt me more than you."

"You won't kill me." He sounded so sure.

"I need her, not you."

Lawrence didn't back down. "Do you really want to start a war with my Pride?"

"They'll never know who killed you because they'll never find your body."

"You don't say," drawled a familiar voice.

Lawrence sighed. "Really, Aunt Lena? I told you I had this."

"Pride security concerns us all." Lena barely spared him a glance as she marched for Lada. "Lada Medvedev, your threat to one belonging to King Arik has been duly noted."

"I can explain," said the now panicking Lada.

"Explain what? That you're a two-timing sow, just like your mother?"

Lada went from apologetic to sneering. "What a surprise, the mighty liger Law needs his aunties to save him."

"Not just his aunts but also a distant cousin." The voice belonged to a stranger, a gorgeous woman with a wicked smile, a handsome guy dressed in all in black by her side.

"Dean. Natasha." Lawrence greeted them. He glanced at Charlotte. "You might recall them as the folks who got married the night we met."

"So this is she." Natasha eyed her up and down. "She's tinier than I would have expected."

Charlotte bristled. "Small is mighty."

"Indeed." The other woman's lips twitched, but her expression was anything but amused as she turned her gaze on Lada. "Naughty bear. Playing games again. Wait until my father hears."

"The Medvedev have no argument with the Tigranov family." Lada looked nervous.

"That's not entirely true now, is it?" Natasha, coiffed and perfect, circled Lada, managing an air of menace that remained elegant as she murmured, "You messed with Lawrence, who is almost a brother to my husband. We are also fairly certain his father was my great-uncle's get. Which makes her"—a manicured finger pointed at Charlotte—"my sister-in-law. By threatening them, you declared war."

"My brother knows nothing of this," Lada huffed.

"Then you better run home and tell him, little bear. Tell the Medvedev sleuth there won't be a place the bears can waddle and hibernate that we won't find. No honey we won't take. No den we won't crush. From here on out, the Medvedev name is to be spat on when spoken."

"You can't do this," Lada exclaimed, looking a bit panicked. "I was just looking for the treasure. I didn't know she was married to Lawrence. And she's human. A human isn't worth going to war over."

Rather than reply, Natasha said, "I'm going to count down from ten. Nine. Eight." By six, Lada's ass was already through the door. At four, Natasha grinned. "Well, that was easier than expected."

Lawrence snorted. "What happened to trying to shed the Tigranov family's mob image?"

"My wife is finding her reputation useful in getting things to move more quickly than regular channels allow." Dean stepped close and glanced at the body on the floor. "Another human. Just like all the guards on the property. What's going on? Your aunts didn't tell us much on the phone, only a set of moving coordinates."

"I should have known they'd call you. I told them I didn't need any help," Lawrence grumbled.

"Stop your whining." Lena flashed him a finger as she returned to the room. "The place is clean. No sign of any other humans."

"Because they never had my brother," Charlotte exclaimed. "It was all a ploy. They wanted to use me to draw him out."

"And why do they need him?" Natasha asked.

That was a question they'd yet to get an answer to. As Charlotte was more properly introduced to Lawrence's best friend and his wife, the aunts took care of the unconscious lady, who was apparently known as Dame Rouge. Given she was passed out, they locked her in a cell in the basement along with her guards. They planned to question her when she regained consciousness. If she ever woke.

Charlotte had hit her really hard.

It was kind of uncanny how at home Lawrence and

the others appeared. They'd gone to exchange a key for her brother, been attacked, and now were drinking wine while lounging in the gaudiest room in existence. Red velvet drapes and overstuffed furniture edged with gold — tassels, leaf, even glossy gold knickknacks.

She paid little attention to the conversation. They passed the key around as if it would suddenly spit out a hologram with all the answers.

But it, like everything else since her arrival in Russia, ended up being another dead end. She still had no idea where her brother was.

Lawrence scooped her up suddenly, "Time for bed."

"Okay." She didn't even argue as she leaned her head on his shoulder. "Wake me when we get to the hotel."

"Fuck the hotel. We're staying here," he said, bounding up the stairs to the second floor.

"Are you sure this is a good idea?" she whispered. "What if more bad guys come?"

"Then I'll eat them."

Her eyes widened.

He smiled. "Just kidding. The only person I plan to eat is you."

And he did so, quite thoroughly.

CHAPTER SEVENTEEN

M aking love to Charlotte that night, then again in the morning, only temporarily forestalled the situation.

Eventually she asked, "When are we leaving?"

There was no point in staying. During the night the people they'd captured had somehow escaped. Apparently, while they slept, Lada rescued them, meaning no answers and an excuse for his aunts to declare a war with the Medvedev family.

Their escape also meant no Peter.

And a mate who still refused to accept him. The only good thing new was her declaration that she was done with Russia.

"If Peter is hiding, then he can find me when he's good and ready," was her sour observation.

"And if he needs your help?"

She shrugged, and he knew it hurt her to say, but she admitted it anyhow. "I think it's become crystal clear I don't have the right kind of skills to do anything."

"Then we'll hire someone who can help."

"I can't afford it."

"I can."

She stared at him. "You know I can't accept it."

"You're my—"

"Mate. Yeah." She sighed. "I want to go home."

"We can leave tonight."

She blinked. "Even if I let you buy me a ticket, I have no passport." She'd seen the ripped-up remains of it when they were going through the destroyed apartment.

"That won't be a problem." He'd pull some Pride strings and get her back to America.

"And what about when we do get back? What then?"

"I'm hoping you give me a chance to prove I can be someone you can count on. I want to get to know you, Charlotte. I think we could be great together."

Had this been spoken in a movie, the heroine would declare her love and they'd kiss and live happily ever after. This was Charlotte.

"I need to think about it."

He didn't dare ask how long it would take her to decide. He made arrangements and got them aboard the Pride jet with others who'd come over to celebrate the wedding. Cousins. Aunts. More aunts. All staring at his Peanut.

Then him.

Then Peanut.

It was Mary-Ellen that finally voiced it. "I bet my candy bar they break up before we reach La Guardia."

Which started the wagering. Through it all, Peanut said nothing, but she did hold his hand and, at one point, did naughtily whisper, "Think they'll go sleep so we can join the mile-high club at one point?"

"No." And he didn't tell her they'd all heard her comment. Privacy didn't exist in the Pride, but cock-blockers did. They made sure the bathroom was kept occupied, meaning the closest he got to Charlotte was her drooling in his lap when she napped.

Eventually, they made it across the ocean, ditched the family, and arrived at his house.

"I expected you to be living in some ultra-modern high-rise," she admitted, entering the restored Victorian.

"That would be my city place." His bachelor pad, which he wouldn't be needing anymore. "This is my country home." Which he also thought of as his forever place. He'd spent the last decade restoring it to its former glory.

She ran her hand over the wooden balustrade that he'd stripped, sanded, and stained himself. "It's beautiful."

"Would it help if I said you're the first woman, other than my aunts, I've brought here?"

"How long before you send me packing?" She slapped a hand over her mouth as if she'd not meant to say it.

"Don't look so horrified. It's a perfectly valid question. A week ago, before I met you, I might have assumed we'd already be done with each other. But..." He shrugged. "Is it wrong to admit I'm just as surprised as you are that when I wake each morning, the first thing I think about, the only person I want to see, is you?"

It sounded dorky spilling from his lips. True. But still super emasculating.

Totally worth it, as it brought a smile to her lips. "I like waking up to you as well, but we have to be realistic. We barely know each other. What happens in a few days or weeks when you tire of me?"

"Shouldn't you be asking what happens if we don't?" He arched a brow.

"Be serious, Lawrence."

He sighed and shoved his hands into his pockets. "I understand your concern. It's not as if my family has been quiet about my reputation, and I earned it. I won't lie. I want you to believe me when I say this is it for me, but that will take time to prove. In the meantime, to help alleviate your concerns, you should know that I've already been in contact with my lawyer. I expect we'll receive the new deed to the house showing you as owner by tomorrow. Also, an account of one million dollars has been established that only you can access."

She gaped at him. "Why would you do that?"

"Because, as some of my cousins pointed out, I am in a position of power right now. You have nothing. No home or funds of your own. In order for you to feel as if you truly have a choice and a say, you need to be in a position where you can walk away."

"I don't need your money or house to say no."

"I know you don't, but I am still giving them to you. Which means, as the owner, you can kick me out right this minute if you want."

"You'd do that for me?"

"We will move as fast or slow as you want." It was his

Aunt Lacey who'd given him that advice. *You can't force her, Roarie. She needs to realize she loves you on her own terms.*

Love? Was that why he felt so utterly torn up?

"What if I wanted you to stay?" The shy invitation filled him with an intense warmth.

"Did I mention the master bedroom has a California king bed?"

"What's wrong with that wall?" She grabbed him by the shirt and shoved him even as she rose on tiptoe seeking his mouth.

He slammed into the plaster, but he'd never been happier. His hands roamed her body, the familiarity of it exciting because he knew where to stroke to make her cry out. He knew how deep and at what angle to have her clutching him tight.

Her mouth was hot and breathless against his. Her legs a vise around his waist and the heat of her molten heaven.

She didn't let him leave that night. Or the next. Or the one after that.

As a matter of fact, they didn't talk about separating at all. Which was what led to the incident with the binder.

CHAPTER EIGHTEEN

It wasn't until two weeks after they'd arrived in America that the binder landed with a thump on the kitchen table, rattling her coffee mug. Charlotte glanced over to see Lacey, hair pinned atop her head, a determined expression on her face.

"How did you get inside?" She knew for a fact she'd set the alarm before going to bed. A bed Lawrence still sprawled in while she got to deal with one of his crazy aunts. They had a tendency of just popping in and not leaving easily.

"I used the front door of course."

"It was locked." Lawrence insisted on it. The attacks might have stopped since they found the key and left Russia, but he worried the danger wasn't over.

"Was it?" Lacey pretended innocence.

Charlotte took a sip of her coffee. "I can see why people put bells on cats."

"And they say we're the ones with claws."

Charlotte scowled. "Maybe I wouldn't be so defensive if I didn't feel as if I was always having to watch myself."

"We wouldn't hurt you."

"Lena showed me a rose bush in the garden and said if I hurt Lawrence, she'd bury me under it."

"Just testing your mettle, dearie. You didn't think we'd let Lawrence fall in love with just anyone, now did you?"

"I would never do anything to hurt him."

"Exactly. Which is why we have some things to discuss," Lacey announced as she dragged a chair close and shoved the big tome closer.

"What is that?" Charlotte had a sneaky suspicion given the hearts and flowers plastered over the cover. In a cutout at the very center was a baby picture of one chubby-cheeked Lawrence and, look at that, in a smaller circle, a picture of Charlotte, cross-eyed.

"This is *the* binder." Lacey beamed as she clasped her hands together. "Shall we begin?"

"Begin what?" asked Lawrence as he entered the room, bare chested and wearing only low-slung track pants. He preferred to be naked, but given it still made her blush when he walked around in the nude, he compromised with bottoms. She would never tire of seeing that vee arrowing from his waist. "Morning, Peanut," he rumbled, pouring himself a cup of coffee.

"Mornin'." She lifted her face for the kiss he dropped on her lips before he sat in the seat across from her.

Two weeks of being domestic and they'd fallen into some habits. The first being that he slept over every night. He'd offered to leave that first day and give her space.

She'd dragged him to bed instead. Nothing she liked more than waking up draped on top of him.

Then it was a quickie in the shower and breakfast before he dropped her off at her new job. He'd helped her find one in a marketing agency that was on the way to his office. However, as he warned, while he was able to give her rides now, if he got sent out of town for work, she'd have to either commute or drive. He'd offered to loan her his lovely red sports car, but she kind of had her eye on his Jeep.

"What is that thing doing here?" Lawrence asked, pointing to the book.

"It's past time we planned the wedding, of course," Lacey said with a "don't be silly" tone.

Charlotte choked on her coffee. "What wedding?"

Lawrence was instantly rubbing her back and took on a stern note as he addressed his aunt. "I don't think this is the right time."

"Why not? It's obvious the pair of you are besotted. Aren't you?"

Lawrence glanced at Charlotte and smiled. "She knows how I feel."

Indeed, she did. He'd told her last night. It started out with them snuggled on the couch watching *The Witcher*. Him growling because she pretended to swoon at the shirtless scenes. It turned into a tickle fight that resulted in her gasping for breath.

"I surrender," she'd finally said.

He'd stilled above her, a heavy weight that teased

rather than crushed. His expression was intent and soft at the same time. It burst out of him. "I love you." He blinked as if surprised he'd said it.

She bit her lip.

He said it again, as if it were a revelation. "Holy fuck, I love you."

What he did after still made her blush. His foot nudged hers under the table.

"And you just proved my point. It is time," Lacey declared.

"That's not up to you." Lawrence shook his head.

Since Charlotte actually liked Lacey, she came to her rescue. "Why do we need a wedding? I thought Lawrence and I were already mated." And as of last night, Charlotte was finally starting to believe it might actually be forever.

Lacey's gaze narrowed. "I have been waiting over thirty years for my boy to settle down. I will have my wedding."

"*Your* wedding?" Lawrence arched a brow. "I'd say if we have one or not, that's up to me and Charlotte, no one else."

Lacey's lower lip jutted. "Just trying to help."

"Do we really need to get married?" Charlotte wrinkled her nose. "Seems like an awful lot of trouble and expense."

Lawrence started to nod, readying to agree, and then he glanced at his aunt, and his expression softened. Just for a second before it hardened. In that moment, Charlotte knew he would choose her over his aunt. He would side with her and break Lacey's heart. She didn't want to be the reason it happened.

Reaching out, Charlotte flipped open the binder and jabbed at the first thing she saw. A wedding dress. "Too much lace." She pointed at another one. "Too poufy." She cocked her head at a third with a square-cut bodice. "I like the top but not the bottom."

Lacey leaned close. "Hmm. Let me show you page ninety-three." As the woman flipped, Charlotte caught Lawrence's gaze over the top of her head.

He mouthed, *Thank you.*

She winked and replied, *You owe me.* Then added, *I love you.*

It was the first time she'd said it, and his eyes widened. His smile exploded, and she thought he might sweep her out of the chair and carry her off. Instead, he dipped close and whispered, "I'll expect to hear those words again tonight."

"Where are you going?" she asked as Lacey pulled out a notepad and took some notes.

"To ask my best friend if he'll stand by my side and book a honeymoon. How do you feel about cruises?"

She would need the vacation apparently because the next two weeks were all about the wedding planning. The venue was booked. It would happen a few hours before the next full moon, a supposedly lucky time of the month.

Only a few things marred the fantasy. First, no sign yet of Peter or the woman who'd kidnapped them twice. Lada had also gone to ground. Second, she stumbled onto the Wedding Pool, which some had rudely nicknamed, the Runaway Groom.

The day she found out, after visiting A Lions' Pride restaurant to get a preview of the menu, she slammed into the house and waved a sheaf of papers. "Do you know what this is!" She stalked in to find Lawrence in his liger shape, jogging on the treadmill set up in the living room so he could exercise while listening to the news.

The graceful feline leaped off the machine and took a moment to shift, distracting her with his naked body before he replied. "What is what?"

"This." She waved the sheets she'd printed out. "There's a betting pool on when you'll try and ditch me before the wedding."

"You don't say."

"People think you're going to get cold feet."

The words no sooner left her lips than he was bracketing her and her back was pressed against the wall.

"And what do you think, Peanut?"

A few weeks ago, she might have doubted and let her anxiety take her for a ride. But she'd gotten to know the man.

She smiled. "I think I'm gonna win a lot of money because I bet on us making at least twenty-five years."

"Only twenty-five?" He leaned in even closer. "I chose fifty."

"You did?" She couldn't contain her surprise.

"I never thought I'd be the kind of man who'd settle for one woman. And then I found you."

"I love you," she whispered, cupping his cheeks.

"Love you more," was his reply as he kissed her.

"Gag me with a spoon. Save it for later, people. You have ballroom dancing lessons in less than half an hour," Lacey announced, walking in and clapping her hands.

"I'm beginning to like your idea of a bell," was his grumbled complaint.

"Three more days," she whispered.

Just three until they married and were on their honeymoon. Without his aunts.

She couldn't wait.

CHAPTER NINETEEN

The waiting killed him. Lawrence paced the nave. Nervous, but not for the reason anyone teased him.

"You still have a few minutes to run," cajoled Lena.

He cast a dark glare at his aunt. "I know about your wager. Really, you think I'd take off five minutes before the wedding and leave her at the altar?"

Lena wore an unrepentant grin. "Guess you're determined to prove me wrong."

"I'm not doing this for anyone but myself. She's the one for me." The one who made him complete, who curbed his urge to roam.

"I'm glad for you, son." Lena kissed him on the cheek.

Then it was Lenore's turn and finally Lacey, who'd gotten her dream wedding minus the horse-drawn carriage. Mostly because the blizzard outside made it unfeasible.

He hugged all three of them, throat tight as he

managed a gruff, "Thank you." For raising him. Loving him. And always being by his side.

His tough aunts pretended it was dust making them teary eyed.

"Damn it all, when was the last time anyone cleaned this place?" Lena wiped the moisture and glared.

How he loved them and could never thank them enough for being there when he needed them most.

Then it was Dean who came to see him, slapping him on the back and saying, "You ready to leave your bachelor days behind?"

He nodded.

"Shall we take our places?"

"I just need a minute."

Dean entered the main part of the chapel and left him alone. Lawrence glanced at his watch then the door.

There was still time.

He couldn't disappoint Charlotte.

The door opened, and his surprise finally arrived.

Lawrence smiled. "About time you showed up."

CHAPTER TWENTY

The aunts arrived only minutes before the ceremony to find Charlotte pacing in her gown, anxious, but not because of the wedding itself. It was going to be beautiful. Lacey had thought of everything, from the blue garter to something old—the key woven into the bodice of her dress—and the new earrings dangling from her ears. The church would be filled with lilies. White ones. Because they were her favorite.

The church was an old one, and an odd choice, yet the aunts insisted it was the perfect location, claiming it had long ago been desecrated by witches. Which made her wonder what kind of surprise they might spring at the ceremony. Blood sacrifice? Would everyone howl at the end?

She had no idea what to expect, and it frazzled her nerves. They didn't improve as a never-ending stream of guests arrived.

All kinds of golden people showed. Even the Lion King, who appeared simply as a man. A handsome one, with a very pregnant woman on one side and a small child on the other. Him, his aunts, his cousins, his second cousins, their families, his friends, all here to see her wed the most elusive bachelor.

"It's almost time." It was Lenore who'd offered to walk her down the aisle in place of the brother she'd never found.

A pang of sadness filled her.

Lacey saw and shook head. "Oh no you don't. No tears allowed."

Sniffling them back, Charlotte tried to regain her composure when suddenly she had three sets of arms around her.

"Don't cry. I swear he's going to marry you!" Lacey promised.

"I know he will," Charlotte hiccupped. "That's not why I'm crying."

"She misses her brother," Lena announced as if they were all too dumb to figure it out.

"'Course she does. No need to bring it up," Lenore snapped.

"We tried to find him, dearie," was Lacey's soft addition.

"I just— just—" Wished she knew if he was at least okay.

They hugged her tighter and let her know without words she wasn't alone.

It made her sob harder, which finally led to Lacey snapping, "Enough with the waterworks. It is go time, people! Someone get me the kit so I can fix her face!"

The hustle and bustle had her laughing as Lacey

turned into a general, repairing her smeared makeup, adjusting her cleavage, and slapping a bouquet into her hands.

As they exited the prep room and entered the hall outside the church nave, the music started as if on cue. Lena clutched her bouquet like she'd throw it at the first person who mentioned the fact she'd worn heels and a dress. She swept through the swinging church doors while Lacey gave last-minute instructions.

"Remember, chin up, tits out, and count to ten before following me." Lacey took her place, shoulders back, beaming, and strode through the doors.

Charlotte trembled, her fist damp around the bouquet. Maybe they should have wagered on her running, because, for a second, she debated it.

Then she thought of Lawrence. The man waiting inside.

The shivering calmed, and she took a deep breath.

Lenore patted her hand. "Thatta girl. Everything will be fine."

Then the woman who was supposed to walk her down the aisle went through the doors and left her alone. The betting pool got it wrong. It wouldn't be Lawrence chickening out today. But her. She couldn't do this. Not alone. Not—

"What the hell, Pumpkin Eater. I leave for six months and come back to you getting married?"

It couldn't be.

"Peter? Peter!" She whirled and threw herself at her brother. The only reason she didn't cry? Because she was livid. "Where have you been? You had me so scared."

She hit him with the bouquet, not caring that petals went flying.

"Whoa. Careful there. I swear I didn't do it on purpose. I got lost in the wilderness. Was sick for a while, and only recently returned."

"I've been looking for you." She sniffled.

"I know, and I'm sorry you were worried. I owe a huge thanks to your fiancé. He managed to track me down."

"I'm glad you're here." Glad he was alive. But she'd be smacking Lawrence later for keeping this a secret. "I want to hear all about what happened. Why was the mob after you? What's the deal with this key?"

He eyed the wrought iron metal woven into her bodice and grimaced. "I honestly don't know and, given what happened to me, not really interested in finding out."

"I don't understand."

"I promise to tell you everything. Later. Right now, I think you have something more important to worry about. You're getting married."

"I am." She nodded.

"Do you love him?" Peter asked, holding her hands, expression intent.

She nodded. "More than anything."

"Then if you're ready, I'd love to walk you down the aisle."

"I'm glad you're here." She clutched his arm as they went through the door. Her smile incandescent as she walked down that aisle to truly become the wife of the liger who loved her.

EPILOGUE

The wedding went off without a hitch, although Lena needed makeup repair. She sobbed throughout the whole thing.

There was even more crying by the single ladies, as yet another eligible bachelor was taken off the market, which meant more than a few eyes lingered on Peter.

As Charlotte slow danced with her husband, she whispered, "Shouldn't we warn him?" Peter had no idea the room was packed with lions.

"Your brother will be fine. Don't worry."

"Easy to say. I haven't seen him in over eight months."

"You can badger him all about his adventures on the cruise."

She paused mid-step to stare at Lawrence. "Wait, he's coming, too?"

"As you stated, you haven't seen him in a long time. I tried to get him here sooner, but there was some red tape

I had to deal with." He'd not been exaggerating when he told Charlotte he had access to better search methods not to mention the funds to release the American being held in a remote jail for theft. Apparently, a very hungry Peter wandered out of the woods and broke into a bakery for food. "I thought it might be nice in between our most excellent lovemaking if you had a chance to catch up."

"You've thought of everything."

"Indeed, I have."

Which was how his aunts ended up on a flight that got cancelled, meaning they missed the boarding call for the boat. And then, when they tried to fly ahead, another favor called in had them delayed at customs. By the time his aunts met them a week later at their last port of call, they were scowling, but it was worth it.

Especially when Charlotte threw up on Lenore's feet and, with a shit-eating grin, Lawrence said, "Guess who's going to be a dad?"

AS LAWRENCE LED A DECIDEDLY green Charlotte away, the aunts crowded around their newest family member by marriage.

Peter.

"We've got some questions for you," Lenore stated.

"About this key." Lena held it up. She'd filched it when Charlotte changed out of her gown for the honeymoon. "Why is it so valuable? What does it unlock?"

"I don't know," was Peter's less than satisfactory

en Lawrence had warned them they couldn't
s mate's brother, she couldn't shake or slap the
boy, but it was tempting.

Lena's irritation emerged in a tense, "What do you mean, you don't know? Your sister got kidnapped by the people looking for it. Hell, you went missing for months because of it."

Peter shrugged. "I wish I could tell you more, but something happened to me while I was lost in that forest in Russia."

"I hear Lawrence had you sprung from prison."

"A misunderstanding."

"How did you end up in there?"

"No idea. The doctors think I might have suffered a head injury since I don't remember much of the last six months."

"Convenient." Lena remarked.

"Too convenient," was Lenore's addition.

And it bugged the curious cats especially since every search they did came up empty, which was why, when Andrei Medvedev reached out to the Lions' Pride, asking how he could repair the damage his sister had wrought, they sent their smartest lioness to meet him, with a simple mission.

Find out why the key was so valuable. And most important, what did it open?

ARE YOU READY FOR THE NEXT WILD ADVENTURE FEATURING A RUGGED RUSSIAN BEAR AND A LIONESS

WHO'S NOT IMPRESSED BY HIS VIRILE NATURE? STAY TUNED FOR **TAMING A BEAR.** AND THEN GET READY FOR PETER'S STORY IN **LION'S QUEST**...BECAUSE AS IT TURNS OUT, HE'S KEEPING SECRETS TOO.

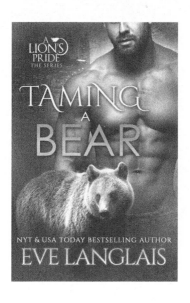

Be sure to visit www.EveLanglais for more books with furry heroes, or sign up for the Eve Langlais newsletter for notification about new stories or specials.

Made in United States
Orlando, FL
11 March 2022

15645495R10118